THE RETURN
OF THE
DRAGON

JANE ZARING

THE RETURN
OF THE
DRAGON

JANE ZARING

ILLUSTRATED BY
POLLY BROMAN

HOUGHTON-MIFFLIN COMPANY
BOSTON · 1981

Printed in the United States of America

P   10 9 8 7 6 5 4 3 2 1

Library of Congress Cataloging in Publication Data

Zaring, Jane T.
The return of the dragon.

Summary: A dragon exiled from his native Wales re-
forms and tries to win the right to return to his home
by doing twelve good deeds in a year.
[1. Dragons – Fiction.   2. Wales – Fiction]   I. Title.
PZ7.Z264Re   [Fic]   81-6258
ISBN 0-395-30350-8   AACR2

FOR DAVID, NOAH, AND PHILIP

CONTENTS

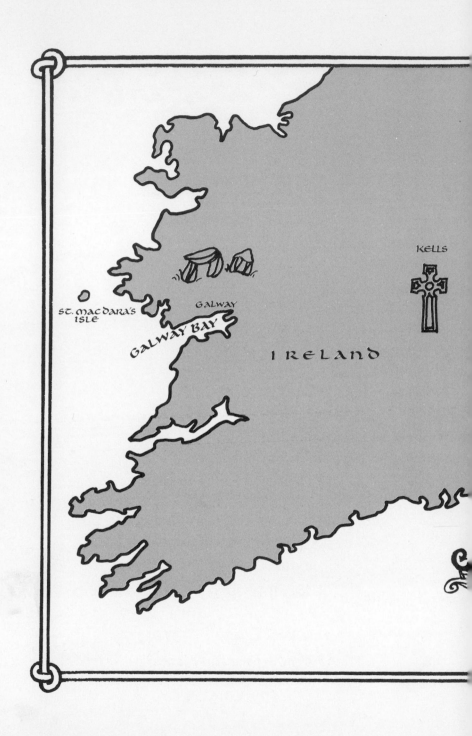

ST. MAC DARA'S
ISLE

GALWAY

GALWAY BAY

IRELAND

KELLS

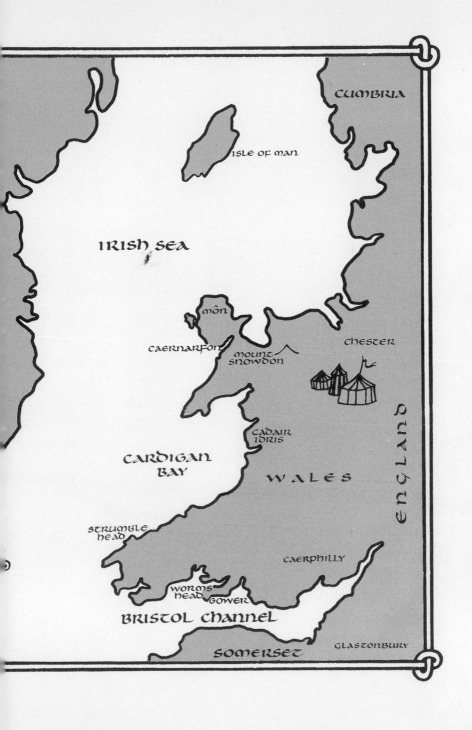

THE RETURN
OF THE
DRAGON
JANE ZARING

CARADOC
RETURNS

O N THE SMALL ISLAND, off the coast of Ireland, there was room for just one Celtic saint and one repentant dragon.

Seven peaceful years had passed since St. Mac-Dara, the hermit, had fished a last-gasp Caradoc out of the Atlantic breakers, and into the safety of his frail leather boat. For seven years the hermit had shared with his dragon guest his knowledge of herbs, remedies, and the amazing lives of the Celtic saints.

"Good heavens!" the dragon, Caradoc, would say as he listened to tales of St. Finian, who ate only stale barley bread and drank only muddy water. Or St. Columba, who drove a water-monster from the River Ness in Scotland. Or St. Brendan the Voyager, who sailed to a beautiful Land of Promise, west of Ireland.

"Good they are, indeed," the hermit would reply gravely.

St. MacDara regarded himself as the least of the host of missionaries, wandering monks, and hermits who had spread Christianity throughout the Celtic world, although not one of the more famous saints could count a dragon among his converts.

In return, Caradoc had enlivened their evenings with stories of his misspent youth.

"Now when I was the terror of all Wales," he would begin, a trifle complacently.

But there was one tale the dragon told his rescuer once. Only once, because he found it too painful to repeat. It was the story of how the townspeople of Caernarfon grew so exasperated with his dragon goings-on that they banded together to drive him out of his home in the cave above the little town, out of the Province of Gwynedd, and right out of the country of Wales. Even now, seven years later, a shiver rang along his bronze scales and the loops of his tail, as he recalled floundering in the Irish Sea while the coast of Wales disappeared in the distance.

Seven years with the good man had been enough

for the dragon to renounce rampaging around the countryside, scorching maidens and parching oats, and to find more sociable uses for his fire. For instance, he had learned to fry fish to a delectable brown. They were both particularly fond of the kippers Caradoc made by smoking herring. Indeed, the hermit found life so comfortable, now that his clothes were always dragon-dry and his cell warm, that he wondered, guiltily, if a little more discomfort would be more pleasing to God. Together they might have got along nicely for the next seventy years, but for one thing: Caradoc was homesick.

He loved the small, damp, upland country where he had grown up, and he found that he simply could not forget Wales. He concentrated on sensible remedies, such as learning every flower and herb in the west of Ireland.

"That'll be the way to put down roots in this Irish turf, begorra." He was working on an Irish brogue.

The hermit smiled an encouraging sort of smile.

Gradually, Caradoc came to like the sound of the waves battering the lonely island. He found a certain beauty in the lichen-covered rocks, and in the Irish mists and rain clouds surrounding them. He made friends with the stormy petrels, black-billed gulls, and seals who also made their home on St. MacDara's Isle. But still the dragon longed for his old home in the cave on the hillside above Caernarfon. Memories of the barren mountain outlines of Snowdon and Cadair Idris haunted him. When he could not sleep, instead of sheep he counted the valleys he knew in Wales. "Twyi, Teifi, Taff," the hermit would hear him rumble. "Rhondda, Rhayader, Rhymney."

"An odd language," thought the hermit, who used Gaelic himself.

One day, as they both rested from the hard work of heaving massive stones into place for the church St. MacDara was building, Caradoc confessed, "I have only to shut my eyes to see my own landscape, instead of this one. The gray stone walls of Caernarfon, and the island of Môn, blue across the silver water of the Menai Straits, are as clear to me as if they were in front of me here. The view from my own cave in that faraway hillside must be the most beautiful sight on earth."

"Then you must go home again," said the hermit with a sigh.

"It is impossible. They drove me out with sticks and stones and catapults and arrows," answered Caradoc miserably.

"Forgiveness from God is freely given, but from mortals it is sometimes possible to earn it—even from the Welsh," said the wise man.

So when, in the seventh summer, a bird sang almost as sweetly as the singing birds in his own country, Caradoc knew he must go back.

The hermit sadly gave his blessing, and a few last sailing tricks, such as whistling up a wind and fading into a mist. Then Caradoc steered the light, leather-hulled boat into the waves of the Irish Sea and headed for Wales.

Whistling up a wind proved a particularly useless piece of knowledge for sailing the western seas. The gales blew nonstop for three days.

"Whistling it down is what I need to know," grumbled the drenched dragon, more green than bronze.

On the third day the gale died down. As the clouds lifted, Caradoc caught sight of land in the watery sunset and made thankfully for the shore.

"What country, friend, is this?" he asked a solitary fisherman.

The man turned pale and gulped like one of his fish. Caradoc thought, too late, that it might have been kinder to try out his ability to hide in a mist.

"Wales, my Lord Sea-Dragon, but we haven't done anything wrong. Indeed to goodness, this is a poor land, with little food to spare and no easy living." The fisherman added, with a faint glimmer of hope, "Perhaps you were looking for England?"

Caradoc was relieved not to have been blown completely off course. He tried to look his most benevolent.

"Man, I will do you no harm. I seek the town of Caernarfon, in the Province of Gwynedd."

The fisherman stopped shivering and looked almost happy. "Oh, that is miles and miles from here. This is South Wales, you know. You want the north."

The dragon, who had had quite enough of the sea by this time, decided to continue his journey on dry land. He handed his boat to the astonished fisherman (known ever after as Jones the Lies) and set out to walk north, toward home.

COMPANIONS

C ARADOC KEPT to the coast, thinking that the fewer people who were alarmed about the return of the last dragon in the Western World, the better. It was a lucky decision. The rain had started again, and the wind blew a soft, salt drizzle from the sea. Caradoc breathed in the moisture-laden air, squelched the sodden turf under his feet, and bubbled with joy. It all felt so right. He began to rumble a tune about the western wind blowing and the small rain falling down. He tramped along contentedly repeating, "The small rain down shall fall," until he paused in his imitation of a rusty kettle to search his memory for another line. In the momentary silence, the wind blew an odd twang to his ears.

He looked around in the mist and darkness. At

first, he could see nothing, but a cautious breath of
fire gave enough light to show him that the sound
came from a harp caught in a rowan tree. The
branches of the tree were just level with the cliff
path Caradoc was walking. Its roots were anchored
in a crevice on the cliff face. On a narrow ledge
below the tree, above a sheer drop to the sea, was
a black lamb, clutching a flag.

When there was nothing else for it, Caradoc
could use his wings. He unfurled them now, and
before long a battered lamb was recovering beside
a Caradoc-fire.

"I was composing my first bardic song and must

have left the path, because I forgot to look where I was going," said the lamb, sheepishly.

"You must sing me the song while we remain by the fire. We can continue our travels by daylight," said Caradoc. It was a generous suggestion. He had planned to travel under the cover of darkness, for he was uneasy about the reaction of people who might catch sight of a bronze dragon tramping through the green Welsh hills.

The lamb, David, sang the song he had composed in honor of his old teacher, David of the White Rock, whose skill was so great that he could teach even a black lamb to play the harp, and whose granddaughter had to lead him around because, although he was the finest bard in all Wales, he was blind. Then David added a poem praising dragon-rescuers. Caradoc privately thought that the lamb had some way to go in barddom. He hoped the dear fellow would find patient audiences.

By morning, David was rather subdued to think his career as a wandering minstrel had all but ended before it had properly begun.

"Where are you going first?" asked Caradoc.

"Generally in that direction," replied the black lamb, with a vague sweep of his hoof northward.

"Then, shall we travel north together?" suggested Caradoc.

David eagerly agreed. They headed inland to a little-used path from the headwaters of the River

Teifi to Mount Snowdon itself.

Caradoc practiced hiding in a mist rather too successfully, so that the two of them walked in a cocoon of gray cloud. It blotted out any distant views they might have had and set Caradoc to musing on all the old familiar places he would visit once more.

Above Tregaron, an old sheepfold loomed up out of the mist. David skipped over to see what he could find among its fallen stones. What he found was a pathetic heap of feathers with the distinctive black and white bars, all darkened now, of a falcon. David called to Caradoc, and together they leaned in dismay over the injured bird. Peregrine, the falcon, opened one filmy eye, saw a black lamb and a bronze dragon, and promptly closed it again.

"I wonder where that poor bird thinks it is?" asked David, as he circled around, trying to provide a woolly windbreak while Caradoc gently breathed warm air over the casualty.

Caradoc tried not to smile in case he let a flame out by mistake. Then, as the lamb watched in admiration, the dragon patiently put to good use the healing skills he had learned when treating St. MacDara's Irish gulls.

"That should do," he said at length, "but who has done you such harm?"

Peregrine raised his head proudly.

"I was th.. favorite hunting falcon of Math, son

11

of Mathonwy, Lord of Gwynedd, and the greatest hunter in the forty cantrefs of the north. Gwern the Wicked grew jealous of our fame. He lured Prince Math to hunt with him in the Forest of Tregaron, where he had hidden three hawks who were to attack me and destroy my skill forever. They left me for dead here, where you found me and saved my life."

"Thank the black lamb there," said Caradoc, nodding at David, whose gaze was fixed on the distant hills as he imagined how splendid the flight of the three wicked hawks would sound on his harp. "Now, until those broken wings mend, you had better ride on my back," the dragon advised.

And so the falcon, Peregrine, whose eyes were so sharp that they could see the moons of Jupiter, or a herring swimming five fathoms deep, and whose wings were so swift that he could dive at two hundred miles an hour like a feathered thunderbolt, joined the journey north.

On the third day Caradoc stopped experimenting with mists. The clouds lifted to show a dimly blue sky overhead. The dragon suddenly felt he must climb to the top of Cadair Idris to catch his first sight of Mount Snowdon. Peregrine was warned of a rough ride ahead. "Forget my bones. They are mending, and I shall be glad to know if my eyes see as far as ever they did," he responded.

David cheerfully scrambled up the trail flattened by the dragon's tail, through the gold of the prickly gorse bushes and the wiry heather, over the springy turf, to where a remote stone barn stood marking the division between the fields and the untamed moorland.

"I am sure your curiosity won't let us pass this place without a look inside, black lamb," said Caradoc, good humoredly.

David nodded until his curly wool danced. And so they turned aside, and it was there they found Rhiannon, the owl, hunched dismally over the chain that fastened her to a perch in the barn entry.

Rhiannon explained that her nest had been

robbed and that she was kept captive in the cruel hope that she would scare away the mice. Five mice darted by, whisking their tails, to prove just how bold they could be when owls were safely tethered.

Caradoc's fire was the perfect tool for melting fetters. The owl was soon freed, but she was curiously slow to fly away.

"I must think where to go. The barn, which was my home, has become unbearable to me since the loss of my owlets and my captivity there."

Peregrine looked at her with understanding. "I, too, am homeless. Now that I have been the hunted, as well as the hunter, I would not return to my old life. Besides," he added sadly, "what place would there be for me now at the court of Math the mighty hunter?"

In the bad old days, Caradoc remembered, princesses were forever blushing and saying in trembling voices to the princes who rescued them from the scaly fate of being captured by a dragon:

> Yours 'til the grave
> Is the life you save.

It tended to unnerve the princes, but nevertheless it seemed now to be the dragon's turn to take care of the lives he had saved.

"Companions," he said, "I am not as single-minded as my friend Saint MacDara, who lives alone, the better to serve God. The bonds of friendship sound good to me. If I am permitted to live once more in the old home I seek above Caernarfon, you are welcome to stay there with me, and to make it your home, too. But I must be honest and tell you that I left many enemies in North Wales, and that I have had little practice in friendship. In truth, the hermit is the only friend I ever had in all my life."

Then he added hopefully, "Until now."

"You are generous," replied Rhiannon. "Surely that is uncommon in a dragon? I would gladly join you, and you shall have such friendship from me as you would wish."

Peregrine lifted a claw. "I give you all my word that you have not seen a truer friend than you will find in me."

David unslung his harp and sang them a sad song about an orphan lamb who wanted a home, which seemed to answer the question.

And so they went on together into the heart of the mountains of Eryri. As Caradoc began to see the familiar landmarks, his pace quickened, and David had to jog-trot to keep up. They rounded the last hill as the sun was setting in a paradise of clouds. Beneath them, Caernarfon was snug on its seashore, and by the long golden light they could see the home cave they sought, empty, wide open, as if waiting for them.

CAERNARFON

B Y THE END of a fortnight's hard work, the
Companions were sitting contentedly outside a clean and well-stocked cave, looking
down on Caernarfon and the ruins of the old Roman
outpost of Segontium.

"Who would live anywhere else in the world
when they could be here?" murmured Caradoc, as
he gazed across the water at the island of Môn,
blue in the distance, and puffed smoke rings for
sheer happiness.

Peregrine, who was proud of his skill and speed
on his mended wings, offered to catch some fish
for supper.

"At least twenty fat herring for me," requested
Caradoc lazily.

"And a clawful of sprats for us," added Rhiannon and David.

Peregrine took off and swooped low over the Menai Straits.

David stood on a rock to watch his flight. Turning back, he saw some unusual movements below him. He looked more carefully and was horrified to realize that the whole hillside was alive with people carrying scythes, swords, pitchforks, hammers, brooms, branches. In fact, anything that would make a weapon. What was more, they were coming toward the cave.

The townspeople of Caernarfon were out dragon-hunting. Not that all of them had actually seen the dragon, but they had certainly heard enough tales of Caradoc's unneighborly nature. Now, they kept up their courage, as they advanced toward the beast's lair, by recalling all they had ever heard of maidens munched, crops flattened, and heroes toppled. It was, they felt, quite unfair that the last dragon in the Western World had reappeared on their doorstep. They hoped to drive him away once more, before he got up to any mischief and before too many people heard of the disgraceful matter. The reputation of being infested with dragons was the last thing Caernarfon wanted spreading through Wales.

When David rushed back with his warning, Caradoc took some deep breaths. He hoped that his most fearsome roars, together with some huffs and puffs of fire, would be enough to scare everyone safely back home. The wise owl, Rhiannon, saw that this was the last thing to do.

"You simply cannot start by making enemies of all our neighbors," she snapped. "I have rarely heard such a feeble-witted idea. We shall never be comfortable here if you frighten them away today. Tomorrow they will just return with more weapons and more volunteers. They will set traps, sprinkle cartloads of dragonquit on your path, and goodness knows what else. And," she added severely, "it is no wonder they are determined to get rid of us, considering the dreadful reputation you earned in these parts."

Caradoc was really rather fond of his tales of that misspent youth and had been telling them to his companions, to cheer up cave-cleaning. Now he stopped mid-rumble, looking abashed.

"You are right. It would be the bad old days all over again."

"What you must do," the owl said more kindly, "is light the biggest bonfire ever seen on this hill."

She dismissed out of hand Peregrine's proposal that he drive back the invaders as if he were hunting with Prince Math.

"No, of course you can't. Have you all taken leave of your senses? We are not dealing with a flock of mice."

This was a very different Rhiannon from the silent, sad bird, given to shutting her eyes and wincing at remembered pain. She sent David scurrying to the potato pile they had spent a week making, and Peregrine hurrying back to his fishing.

The attackers were chilled with fear and soaked by the drizzle, which had been falling all day. The nearer they got to the dragon's den, the more sinister it seemed. They bravely struggled on until, suddenly, they stopped and sniffed. The most delicious smell imaginable was wafting down the hill: succulent herring and potatoes frying to a crisp brown.

Every man and boy there felt that nothing had ever made them more hungry than this business of dragon-hunting. So when a particularly harmless black lamb invited them to join the feast around the fire, it was more than cold, wet, hungry flesh could resist. Putting down their weapons in twos and threes, and then in tens and dozens, the dragon-slayers came to supper.

After the meal, a reluctant spokesman for the people of Caernarfon was pushed forward by his fellows. "Harrumph." He fixed his eyes on the pile of fishbones, so as not to have to look directly at Caradoc, and cleared his throat once more. "Harrumph." The crowd shifted nervously, wondering what happens when you say no to a dragon.

"It's like this, you see. No offense meant, but we were all wondering when you would be leaving these parts."

He paused, being by nature a kindly and hospitable man. His sense of duty, and three townsfolk, prodded him on.

"You tell us you've mended your ways. Maybe that's true. Maybe it isn't. But we remember the old troubles, and you won't catch us risking a dragon neighbor. That's flat."

Embarrassed at being so unfriendly after enjoying the dragon's good meal, he allowed, "I will say one thing, though. You fed us right royally tonight. We'd like to thank you for the best fish and chips we've tasted in many a long year. Now, seeing how spic and span you've made the cave, we suggest that you spend a day or so here before moving on. We wouldn't even object to a week, providing that was all."

There was a general murmur of agreement. Peregrine, fiercely loyal to Caradoc and feeling Caernarfon ought to be honored by his return, rose into the air as if to dive into the midst of the crowd in his best thunderbolt fashion. Rhiannon, who had seemed asleep, snapped one eye open. Peregrine caught her look and promptly changed his plans, digging his talons deep into an inoffensive oak branch instead.

David wondered anxiously what a proper bard would do in the situation. Of course! He would soothe hard feelings with soft music and play until the dragon-slayers sat down with the lamb and cheered for the return of Caradoc the Exiled. He reached for his harp, but the only song he could remember celebrated the rescue of a gentle Welsh maiden from a fearsome dragon. David's eagerness to help was sometimes stronger than his common sense, but even he thought it better not to sing that one.

Caradoc broke the uneasy silence by leaning forward and making a great business of blowing the fire into a brighter blaze.

"I would remind you that I am Welsh, too. This is my country. I was homesick for these hills. They are well named the Mountains of Longing. But I cannot repeat the bad old days and live here in a state of warfare with you. Believe me, you see a different dragon from the one who used to make life difficult for you. Give your consent to my remaining here, and I give you my word that you will never regret it."

"A dragon's word? As well believe a unicorn," snorted someone at the back of the crowd. Unicorns are well known for adjusting the truth until it makes the prettiest picture.

The jeer released a storm of protest.

"If we let them stay, our wives won't sleep."

"The children will have nightmares."

"The wells will run dry."

"The milk will curdle."

"Our young men will spend hours turning their plowshares into swords, and who will have time to carve love spoons?"

"To say nothing of what will happen to the harvests."

"Drive him out."

"Send him to England."

"Better put them all in a boat to sail west for Saint Brendan's Land of Promise. That should take care of 'em."

Caradoc bore the protests with the patience the Irish saint had taught him, but Peregrine could not stand this criticism of his friend. His feelings boiled over in his harshest hunting cry, which had the effect of riveting everyone's attention on him.

"At the court of Math, son of Mathonwy, there are many skilled doctors, but none so skilled as Caradoc the Dragon. Have you taken leave of your senses, people of Caernarfon, that you drive away the student of Saint MacDara, the greatest healer in all Ireland? Besides," he offered, less fiercely, "my sight was counted the keenest in the forty cantrefs of the north. I could keep watch over your shores and warn you of the approach of enemies."

Several people looked thoughtful.

"Something in that. It'd be grand to have a bit of an early warning of Viking raiders."

"Do you think he can cure warts and all?"

"My old woman does have this everlasting backache."

"I don't think there is a good healer in all Gwynedd."

A voice broke into the uncertainty, saying loudly, "Allowing that dragon back in the Province, when we thought we had got rid of him once and for all? We shall be the laughingstock of Wales!"

Opinion, which had become kinder to Caradoc, swung against him again. People glanced back to where their weapons were piled at the edge of the circle of firelight.

"Give a dragon an inch and he'll take a mile, is what I always say. No use expecting a dragon to change his scales."

"That's so. Don't never trust no hawks, neither."

"Right. They'll scare away the fish."

David was still ransacking his mind for the right song. He plucked a few chords on his harp to coax his memory. The crowd fell silent and looked at him expectantly. He clearly had to do something, and almost before he knew it, he was pouring out the story of the last few days in a half-talk and half-chant, plucking a few random strings whenever he needed to draw breath.

Surprisingly, it was favorably received. The Welsh pride themselves upon being a musical nation, so the people of Caernarfon prepared to welcome any pupil of the great bard, David of the White Rock, even though this particular pupil seemed a trifle out of the ordinary.

"Funny style of singing, these newfangled bards have. I prefer the old way myself."

"I like a bit of a song now and then. Perhaps the black lamb would oblige at weddings and such?"

"Did you hear what he said about that dragon being the kindest, gentlest creature in Christendom?"

"Can you credit it? Of course, Celtic saints do have a way with miracles."

The opposition to Caradoc's returning to his old haunts seemed to be wavering again. Rhiannon decided it was time for events to be guided by an owl. She opened both eyes and said, very distinctly, "Hot water."

The crowd blinked at her in puzzlement. Coolly, she explained.

"In January, when your water freezes hard, think

how much a single breath from a well-intentioned dragon could aid you ice-chippers."

It was a telling blow. The people of Caernarfon had their ideals of agreeable neighbors and a peaceful life, but notions of comfort can creep into daily life more frequently than ideals. The lure of reduced winter chores was powerful.

Rhiannon took the offensive. "What will convince the good people of Caernarfon that the dragon they see before them is a new creature and worthy to live in this province?"

No one had a good answer. There were uneasy mutterings. Caradoc caught snatches of "dreadful reputation" and "hundreds of bad deeds." He faced his critics squarely and replied to the last comment.

"Would a hundred good deeds, then, suffice to wipe out old memories and prove Saint MacDara's convert is in earnest?"

"Fifty would be enough," said the first spokesman, willing to meet him halfway.

"I reckon we should settle for twenty," said a man with a sore shoulder.

"A round dozen would convince me," said someone who hated the cold.

David had lost track of the proceedings. A suitable song seemed at long last to be hovering near the tips of his curly black wool. Rhiannon continued to see reason for an owl to take charge. She flapped her great wings. Her luminous eyes dared anyone to disagree.

"Tu whit. How wise the people of Caernarfon are. Tu who. To settle the matter in this fashion."

The said people looked a little stunned to find they had managed to settle the matter wisely, but owls know about wisdom, so they listened as she went on.

"Your verdict, then, is that Caradoc can prove his repentance, atone for old wrongs, and earn his right to live in his old home beside your delightful town by doing twelve good deeds."

David, who was a bit baffled by the sudden interest in numbers, caught the word "twelve" and was flooded with memories of the joyful Minstrels' Feast David of the White Rock held on the Twelfth Day of Christmas each year. The elusive tune came at last. His hoofs lightly moved over a happy Twelfth Night song that soon had people smiling and congratulating one another for arriving at the right solution to the dragon problem.

"Harrumph."

"Caradoc can do something for that throat," murmured Rhiannon from behind half-closed eyes.

"I'd appreciate that," said the spokesman, feeling his natural kindliness comfortably take over again. "Murrumph. Never let it be said that this town turned away a returning son — er — native beast without good reason. Why not stay in your old cave — on approval, mind — for a twelvemonth? Say until next Twelfth Night, as in the song that lamb is singing?"

And so it was settled. Caradoc had until Twelfth Night a year hence to demonstrate by twelve good deeds that there was a new kindly dragon in the cave above Caernarfon. If he managed to do that to the satisfaction of all the townsfolk, then he would be allowed to stay as long as he wanted in the place he loved.

"Companions," the dragon said gravely that night, when he, Rhiannon, Peregrine, and David were at last alone, "if I have managed to serve you, you have done no less for me. Without your help I should be an outcast at this moment. Truly, friendship is a great gift."

"Don't feel too much in our debt," said Rhiannon.

"Remember, we were fighting for our home, too. Besides, I never thought to find life so interesting again."

"Don't thank me," said Peregrine. "I never did anything half as exciting with Prince Math."

"I shall compose a new song for each deed," announced their resident bard. "But will you all help me to remember them at the right time?" David smiled confidingly around the firelit group.

CHE BLACK WICCH

THAT SPRING was a bleak one along Cardigan Bay. Not a fish was caught from Lleyn to St. David's in January and February. By March, everyone was hungry.

"Indeed to goodness, there has never been so little to cook in my time, nor in my mother's time, nor even in my grandmother's time," an old woman told Rhiannon.

Luckily, there was food growing in the Companions' garden. Still, they all agreed with Caradoc, who grumbled, "Cabbage raw, cabbage fried, and cabbage boiled. From breakfast to supper, we eat nothing but cabbage. It is quenching my fire and turning me green and leafy."

Rhiannon varied the menu to Cabbage-with-

Leek on Sundays and threatened Cabbage Surprise (made with toasted earthworms) on Mondays.

"Do you think taking a potful of boiled cabbage down to the hungry in Caernarfon would be counted a good deed?" asked David. "It might be one way to get rid of the stuff."

"Not if they all get indigestion," rumbled Caradoc.

Peregrine reminded David of the evenings when Caradoc had gently browned juicy, fat herring over the fire.

"I doubt if we shall ever sniff that scrumptious smell again," he predicted glumly.

Cabbage and seaweed were steaming on the fire one blue, blowy March day, when a dismal group struggled up the hill. Caradoc's reputation as a healer had spread throughout North Wales, and they had come from Aberdovey, a fishing village on Cardigan Bay, to beg him to return with them and cure an outbreak of spring-sickness there. Caradoc readily agreed to do what he could. So after resting from their journey and drinking some bowls of nourishing (and in David's opinion, quite disgusting) soup, the fishermen set out with the Companions for Cardigan Bay.

In Aberdovey it was plain that the men, women, and children were sick largely because they did not have enough to eat. Caradoc's medicines soon cured the fever, but the people were still listless and weak from hunger and likely to fall ill again.

The Companions puzzled over what lasting help they could give.

Every day Caradoc would search for the seaweeds, roots, and herbs that the old Celtic saint had taught him were good to eat. He passed on his knowledge to the villagers, who learned where to find them for themselves. At least it put some meager food on their tables.

"I suppose teaching like that must be a good deed?" asked Peregrine, who would have liked Caradoc to do something more dramatic.

"No, merely a duty," replied the dragon.

Every day, too, Rhiannon would investigate hollow trees for wild honey. She mostly found squirrels' forgotten stores of moldering acorns, but once or twice she was lucky. And every day Peregrine would fly, unhopefully, farther and farther out to sea, in case his keen sight could spot the missing shoals of herring.

Returning from his endless errand one evening, he pounced on a crab that had failed to scuttle beneath a rock in time. But Peregrine's hope of crab supper promptly vanished as his captive waved its pinchers and snuffled, "Let me go, and I will tell you why there are no fish in the bay."

Peregrine agreed, and in a most peculiar reedy whine the crab intoned:

Black is the work on Strumble Head
Where monsters eat the fisherman's bread.

31

The crab would say no more; Peregrine could only thank it politely and return it, a little gingerly, to a rock pool. Then he took the strange rhyme back to his friends. It made no sense to any of them.

"At least one thing is clear," said Caradoc at last. "If we hope to end the famine in Cardigan Bay, we must go to Strumble Head."

They said farewell to the people of Aberdovey and set out along the coast. Their journey was not cheerful. In every village they came to, the story of hunger and empty fishing nets was the same. A full moon was rising as the cliffs of Strumble Head came into sight at last. They were all tired from the long day's journey. Rhiannon suggested a stop, but Caradoc objected.

"No, we must not stop now. This is the very night for Black Work, whatever that might be."

So they gave up the enticing idea of a cave, a

fire, and a sleep and moved closer to the towering headland.

As the moon reached its zenith, a great marmalade-and-black cat stalked the skyline, followed by a chilling figure, whose dark cloak blew strangely in the wind.

"The Black Witch of Carmarthen. I should have known," breathed Rhiannon.

David tried to stop the shivers he felt at the name.

The witch gave a shrill, strange call into the wind.

"Der-ywch, der-ywch, der-ywch."

Down the silver path of moonlight churned a monstrous jumble of claws, shells, legs, and feelers. Tidal waves surged around the bay as the creatures thrashed the water at the base of the cliffs.

The witch shook a few drops from her flask over one armored back and, in a voice that turned David's stomach upside down, cawed, "That's for you, my little stinging nettle."

The monster, already the size of a cow, grew as big as a whole cowshed.

She aimed at the second. "That's for you, my lovely spinach leaf."

The monster grew bigger than Caerphilly Castle.

"And that's for you, my adorable stinking lousewort."

The third monster swelled to the size of Eglwysilan Mountain.

"Now, my chickens," she screeched. "Go and

swim, up and down, down and up. Be vigilant. Be quick. Do not let a single fish escape your tentacles."

The outrageous creatures swam back down the moonpath and out into Cardigan Bay.

The witch clambered back along the cliff path to her home among the deserted hut circles, the cat picking its way behind her.

"Aha, Mog," she said to her familiar. "Soon everyone along this coast will be so hungry that for the sake of a few fish they will do exactly as I command. You and I, my dark Prince of Cats, will rule Wales, and after that, Cornwall, then Cumbria, then Scotland. We will stop only when the whole

Island of the Mighty is ours, my marmalade Moggy. We will be the most powerful pair in the Western World, thanks to three overgrown shellfish."

Saying this, she stowed the flask of green liquid under a great Standing Stone of blue granite, watched by Rhiannon, whose eyes were particularly good in the dark.

"We must guard our enlarging potion well, Mogkins, because when this is gone there is no more."

Caradoc was not a magician, but one of the things his old friend, the hermit, had taught him was how to reduce things to their proper size. All next day he simmered and stewed. He chanted tuneless chants and sent the others out to gather marsh samphire, whose chief property seemed to be a fearsome smell, lesser mugwort, touch-me-not, pussy willows, and clawfuls of seaweed.

"Nothing in the world would make me taste that," said David firmly, looking at the green sludge Caradoc was stirring, alarmed that it might be tried out on him.

Eventually Caradoc distilled some crystal-clear drops from the muddy mixture and was satisfied.

The last birds had stopped singing, and the badgers had come out of their setts to play, when Rhiannon flew to the hut circles on her noiseless wings. She found the hidden flask with her talons and emptied it over the Standing Stone. The Stone was too old and too deeply rooted in other times to do more than grow a little in stature, until she stood as tall as her sisters at Stonehenge. Rhiannon filled the container with Caradoc's concoction and replaced it.

At the next full moon, the witch again stood at Strumble Head, holding the flagon full of what she thought was her own green brew.

"Der-ywch, der-ywch, der-ywch" sounded out again over the sea. When the three giant humps broke the water, she dropped Caradoc's cold, clear drops on each ugly lump.

The effect was remarkable. The giant creatures shrank, instantly, to three ordinary shrimp. Frightened by all the commotion, they scampered into an old crab shell to hide.

Soon there were plenty of fish in Cardigan Bay. In Aberdovey and in the cave above Caernarfon, everyone sniffed the mouth-watering smell of fresh mackerel cooking for supper and knew that nothing in the world could ever smell as good.

"Eleven to go," announced David, tuning his harp.

"No, no," protested Caradoc. "This deed was not mine. It belongs to all of us."

"Eleven to go," repeated Rhiannon firmly.

On Strumble Head, all that spring and summer, a strange old woman in a black cloak, watched by her marmalade cat, muttered of lost riches and forgotten spells as she poured every imaginable green liquid over the waves. Whenever she did, unnoticed below, three little shrimp huddled together and hid under a frond of seaweed.

CHESTER FAIR

I T WAS THE LAST, best day of April. David had gone hop, skip, and jumping down to Caernarfon for the joy of being alive. Peregrine listened to a pair of curlews deciding on a nesting place. Caradoc rested his eyes with pleasure on a clump of primroses, pale yellow beside his rhubarb patch, and postponed his plan of scouring the island of Môn for somebody in need of a good deed. Rhiannon was taking her customary daytime nap, high in the back of the cave. This peaceful scene was shattered by David, bouncing back, full of a brilliant notion.

"We're all going to Chester Fair tomorrow. We'll take some food and start within the hour," he announced.

"They will treat us as another side show," warned Caradoc.

"Wisdom tells me that, tu who," murmured the owl, "but black lambs convince one that there are times to be foolish."

The May Day Fair was famed far and wide for its pies and gingerbread, its maypole dancing and tightrope walking, its commotion of shepherds and milkmaids, its wandering tinkers and Gypsies, its performing bears and its indescribably exciting bustle and din. Now that they came to think about it, it seemed to the Companions the only place to go. So they set out on their journey in high spirits and eventually arrived outside the walls of Chester, along with most of North Wales.

It was indeed a splendid day. The crowd accepted the Companions as part of the entertainment and cheered as they went by. It was disconcerting at first, but Peregrine soon found he was enjoying himself enormously and giving more royal waves back than ever Prince Math, son of Mathonwy, had. By evening, agreeably tired and stuffed with gingerbread, they drifted to the West Gate to start the journey home. Outside the gate some curious, round tents had gone up during the day. They followed the crowd toward them.

"Those must be the Travelers from Tartary with this here Wild Beast Show," said one bystander, nudging another as the Companions went by.

Caradoc overheard and turned away, shaking his bronze scales. But David still had a penny burning to be spent and an irresistible itch to see inside. He paid his money, slipped in, and saw, too late, why Caradoc had objected.

The animals were all huddled in small, smelly cages, reeking of misery. There was a four-horned, spotted, Himalayan wild goat, which looked remarkably tame. An unmoving snake was said to be the most poisonous in Turkestan, so no one came too close. There was a small black bear from Outer Mongolia, irritably rattling its chain. A talking Tartar dog wore a nomad's felt collar and yelped at intervals, "Greetings from Genghis Khan." His eyes met David's with a beseeching glance. Through the entrance of the next tent, David could see a despondent eagle ("straight from the slopes of Mount Everest, friends").

The triumph of the sad collection was in the last tent, striped gaudy red and yellow, which opened, with a flourish and a rattle of wooden clackers, to reveal a real, live unicorn. The unicorn's ribs stuck through her yellowed coat. She stood with her head down. Her horn, all fluted like a spike of sugar, pointed at the ground. David could feel the sadness seeping out of her. He tried to say something cheerful, but she would neither look nor answer. Some of the crowd tried to poke her into action with sticks, and her despairing look sent David straight out of the Wild Beast Show in search of the Companions.

Caradoc, Rhiannon, and Peregrine could scarcely believe that a genuine unicorn was on show in a grubby tent at Chester Fair.

"But there is only a handful of them left in the world. They are almost as rare as dragons," objected Caradoc.

"Perhaps it was a pony with a false horn," suggested Rhiannon kindly.

"Or a white mule in fancy dress," offered Peregrine.

But David's certainty, and his distress, shook them. Rhiannon undertook to see for herself as soon as it was dark.

The unicorn remained dumb with misery when

the owl flew into the tent. Rhiannon just had time to see that this undoubtedly was the real thing before three people came into the tent. She flitted into the shadows at the top. Hidden there, she discovered that they were Welsh Tartars from the Rhymney Valley, not the Central Asian kind at all.

"This miserable beast gives me the pip," said one.

"How's that?" asked the second.

"A bag of bones is all she is, look you," said the first. "Can't get her to eat for love nor money. Next thing you know, she'll die on our hands, and then we'll be up to our necks in trouble. The English always make a right royal fuss about cruelty to dumb animals."

"And stuffed unicorns don't pull in the same crowds," sympathized the second.

"Ever heard of Powdered Unicorn Horn?" asked a third voice with excitement and greed mixed together.

"Can't say I have."

"You will, mun, you will. The stuff's going to make our fortunes. Listen here: you think of it, and Unicorn Horn cures it! One dose gives back lost youth, strength, or hair. Take your pick."

"Strewth. What'd two doses do?"

"Now you're talking. Two doses bring total happiness and a lifetime's freedom from hiccups. You can use it to bend pokers, fall in love, or cure warts."

"What'll it cost if it does all that?"

"Aha! Powder of Unicorn Horn is the most costly cure you can buy. And we are going to capture the market with the horn of this gloomy beast and live in luxury for the rest of our lives. Think of it. We could buy Caerphilly Castle as a summer home."

There was a silence as the lovely idea sank in.

"What's more," he added, "after we have sawn off the horn, we can always sell the unicorn as a work pony or pack horse, if she survives."

With that they moved on, leaving the unicorn trembling and bleating in a pitiful tone, "I shall die and nobody will save me."

"Courage," murmured Rhiannon, flying low. "We will rescue you."

But the unicorn just whimpered hopelessly.

The Companions knew that by morning the Wild Beast Show would have packed up and moved on, so they must be quick.

"We can never do it in the time," said Peregrine, but his sharp eyes had seen the key to the chained animals. He went to purloin that, if he could. David hastened to find a honey-seller and buy all the stock she had left. Rhiannon, who often thought in feathers, wedged at the top of the unicorn's prison a bolster she had found in the fake Tartars' sleeping quarters.

Caradoc began by melting the chains of the talking dog, the goat, and the Mongolian bear. Peregrine returned in triumph with the key and freed the eagle, while Caradoc started breathing fire on the triple-thick chains that bound the unicorn's cage.

"I said no one can save me," bleated the dismal unicorn, seeing the other captives were already free.

"Now, don't be feeble," said Rhiannon at her sharpest.

The little brown dog could hardly contain his joy. David popped a large blob of honey into his mouth to divert his mind from yelps of delight, but he could still be heard muttering thickly something that sounded like:

> O frabjous day!
> Callooh! Callay!

The mountain goat used his freedom to butt everyone in sight. The snake turned out to be stuffed. The bear single-mindedly demanded, "More honey." Despite the Companions' plans for a silent rescue, there was soon a fair hubbub.

The unicorn's chain was still resisting Caradoc's fire when a jailer came in to investigate the commotion.

"Help!" he yelled. "The animals are free."

His fellows followed fast, armed with sticks and

whips and a noisy determination to have all their captives back under bolt and bar.

The eagle, who had a score to settle, started the fray by diving on her captors and driving them back with beak, wings, and talons. Rhiannon slashed her bolster, and, hidden by the cloud of feathers, the unicorn's chain gave way at last. The so-called Tartars, desperate not to let their dreams of a fortune escape, rushed to the attack again.

Another swoop by Peregrine, Rhiannon, and the eagle drove them back, fearing that a squadron of eagles had come to fight. The goat ran for freedom, butting anyone he found in the way. After him the bear, who was looking for more honey, barged a way clear out of the tent toward that precious sweetness. The talking dog kept calling "over here" from unlikely corners. The dark, the din, and the feathers everywhere were confusing enough for the animals to get safely away. All except the snake, and that was just as well.

Under the peaceful stars of the Welsh night, Caradoc swirled a small mist, as St. MacDara had taught him, to hide them from pursuit. Then the eagle gravely thanked the Companions, offered to come if ever they needed her, and soared back to her old eyrie in the Brecon Beacons — mountains in South Wales, not Asia, it turned out. A kind girl called Mary, whom they met on the sands of the River Dee, restored the unicorn's spirits somewhat by making her a garland of kingcups and telling her how beautiful she was. The goat turned out to be a Welsh mountain goat and decided to live on Snowdon. The Companions, who had not taken to his smell nor his manners, rather wished he had chosen somewhere more remote, though they later changed their minds about that. The bear took off, without even a thank-you, in the hopes of finding more honey. The Companions never heard of him again.

The unicorn was so in the habit of unhappiness that she proved a depressing companion. They managed to cheer her a little by making a special detour to let her wash her mane and gaze at herself in the clear waters of the most beautiful lake in North Wales, Llyn Perys. The unicorn was rather vain of her silky white coat and her silver horn.

How she was smuggled back to her own hidden pool, painted brown, with Peregrine and Rhiannon hiding her horn whenever they passed a stranger, is another story.

But the best thing of all was that the curly brown dog, Japhet, turned out to be the most endearing and merry of friends. When the Companions heard his story — how he had been homeless since he was stolen from Mount Ararat as a puppy, by Gypsies traveling through Turkey — they invited him to make his home with them, in the snug cave above Caernarfon. They were to argue, for many months afterwards, whether a deed that brought them so much pleasure, in the shape of the lovable Japhet, could truly be counted as good.

"After all," said Caradoc, always fair, "we did take away the livelihood of those Gypsies, or Tartars, or whatever they call themselves."

"Stuff and nonsense," said Japhet stoutly. "It was the best deed seen this year between Mount Ararat and Mount Snowdon, taking the long way round."

"Don't convince *me*; convince the good people of Caernarfon," said Rhiannon, so softly that no one listened.

ᴄhe sᴄoɴe
ᴄoɾaᴄle

O NE EVENING in May the Companions sat on their hillside, listening to the first cuckoo calling in the valley and watching the wind stir the host of golden daffodils by the water below. "I am going to remember this always," said Japhet, "because nothing could be better, not even Turkish tulips." Caradoc puffed the fire into a cheerful blaze, and they all ate an enormous supper of fish and chips. Afterward, David, remembering something Caradoc had said in Chester, asked, "Caradoc, when did you last meet another dragon?"

"Seventeen years ago," he answered, finishing off a kipper pudding that only he would eat, "and seventy years would be too short before I met that miserable beast again."

"Tell us about it," demanded the others.

So Caradoc told them about the Korean dragon: how he had ravaged the countryside from Vladivostok to Omsk and Tomsk, and how Caradoc had eventually driven him back with a huge counterfire.

"It worked, certainly, but it left one entire side of the Ural Mountains scorched," said Caradoc ruefully.

"I think it recovered," said Japhet, who had been around.

"Did you ever hear of him again?" asked Peregrine.

"Yes, I did. The next time he was even more troublesome," said Caradoc.

Then he told how the Korean dragon had turned up in Tibet, burning crops and villages and terrorizing the whole country.

"But that time I stopped him for good," said Caradoc rather smugly.

"How?" asked Japhet, hoping the story would go on and on. Japhet dearly loved storytelling.

"I doused his flame with some wet seaweed and rancid yak butter and a spell or two. Now he huffs and puffs sheer wind and can never trouble anyone again."

"Never is a long time," muttered Rhiannon.

In the odd way that hearing something once soon makes it crop up again and again, May was not over before news reached Caernarfon of a fearsome dragon rampaging into Europe from the Northeast. Dreadful tales were told of the havoc it had made in Finland, the crops destroyed in Latvia, the Polish villages left smoldering in its wake. At last some migrating birds brought Rhiannon the whole story of how the Korean dragon had persuaded the Wise Woman of the Samoyed to relight his fire and was blazing a trail toward Caernarfon and his revenge.

Caradoc was greatly distressed to be the unwilling cause of such destruction. He knew well that to quench the dragon's fire a second time would take something far more powerful than overripe Menai butter and damp Welsh seaweed. It would take something beyond his skill.

"I could ask the hermit, but Saint MacDara knows more about good than evil," he said.

"The Sibyl of Iceland might know how to do it," mused Rhiannon.

"Who is she?" asked David.

"The wisest woman in the West," Rhiannon replied, "though I understand she says now that she is too old to be disturbed and refuses to see people."

After a long night of anxious discussion, the Companions decided the Sibyl was their only hope, so they borrowed a boat at Caernarfon harbor and off they sailed, through the spring storms, to Iceland.

Caradoc made sure that news of their departure

reached the Korean dragon. The news had the desired effect; instead of burning its way west across Britain's green and pleasant land, the dragon set sail from Antwerp in red-hot pursuit.

The Sibyl lived at Thingvellir in the middle of Iceland. She was not pleased at having visitors, and when the Companions struggled across trackless lava fields to her sod-roofed cottage, she firmly shut the door. It opened just a crack when David played her the most beautiful of all songs of the blind bard, David of the White Rock, and a crack more to watch Japhet juggling dizzily with three gull's eggs. She grudgingly put out a hand to accept, from Caradoc, a small, purple selfheal plant for her herb garden, and was about to shut the door again when Rhiannon gave her a bunch of white heather she had gathered on the mountain slopes of Snowdon. The old woman's eyes filled with tears as she remembered gathering heather on Snowdon herself, as a girl long ago, before she came to Iceland. When she had recovered, she gruffly said, "Tell me your request. If I can help you, I will."

Then Caradoc told her of all the havoc the Korean dragon was wreaking and of the need to stop him once and for all.

"Long, long ago," said the Sibyl, "they sent for me from Greenland, where I did manage to extinguish the fire of a fearsome old Viking dragon."

Japhet threw all three eggs in the air at once with delight that the Companions had come to the right place.

"But even if I could remember that spell, I no longer have the necessary ingredients," she went on.

Three eggs smashed.

"What do you lack?" asked Rhiannon, ignoring the mess.

"I must have the leaves and roots of the lesser dragonbane. It is a plant that grows now only on the island of Tristan da Cunha."

"In the South Atlantic?" asked Caradoc in dismay.

"Three thousand miles from here," echoed Rhiannon.

"Then it is hopeless," said Peregrine flatly.

"I can show you a quick route to Mongolia, if that would help," offered Japhet, ever hopeful, but weak on geography.

"I can help you in one way," said the Sibyl. "In return for the memory of my girlhood, I will gladly give you my boat. I am an old woman now, and do not use it. It will carry you swiftly to the southern waters."

The boat had been put away many years before. Caradoc melted it out of its safe hiding place under the ice of the Vatnajökull glacier, and the Companions looked at it with dismay. It was a coracle, the light boat that fishermen in Wales carried easily on their backs from one lake to another but rarely used to go venturing in the Atlantic gales. But the quite incredible fact about it was that it was made out of stone. (Japhet knocked it to make sure.) Around its edge were ancient runes, whose secret the Sibyl whispered to Rhiannon. Heaving it into the water, they all felt how unlikely was the prospect of ever getting out to sea, let alone to the South Atlantic, where the remote island of Tristan da Cunha lay. But, as the Sibyl had foretold, the stone coracle floated high as a cork on the waves.

"You must stay," the Sibyl said to Caradoc. "The ground already shakes with the coming of your enemy. Your friends must be quick, or they will be too late."

Rhiannon found the right runic symbols to rub. The amazing craft turned and then sailed true as a die and light as a feather, south toward Tristan da Cunha, leaving Caradoc to face the Korean dragon.

He wasn't long in coming. Spitting flames a full forty yards, the Korean dragon came storming to meet Caradoc.

Now, Caradoc had placed himself carefully. When his adversary caught up with him, he was perched high on the Vatnajökull glacier. The more fury and flames the Korean dragon spat, and the more hot air he hurled across the ice, the faster the glacier melted. In avalanches of loosened ice and torrents

of melted water the dragon from the East grew wet, cold, and extraordinarily cross.

It took the Korean dragon two days to stop wheezing and coughing and begin another attack. This time Caradoc began to wonder rather desperately how long he could hold out. Raising mists from melting ice, dislodging boulders, and slithering down rock screes could not go on indefinitely.

Meanwhile, Peregrine had been taking anxious sightings in the South Atlantic.

"No land yet. Nothing but water, water everywhere," he reported.

"What happens if we miss the island?" asked David.

"One thing is certain: you, my lamb, will find yourself playing the harp to penguins in the Antarctic," snapped Rhiannon, who did not quite trust the strange boat and was worried about Caradoc. She knew that his fighting skills had not been used since St. MacDara had taught him to love peace. If they could not find the dragonbane, the Korean fire-eater would surely overcome the kindly dragon of the West.

But the stone coracle made no mistake. It did not stop until it sped surely to the green cliffs and black beaches of Tristan da Cunha itself.

Landing was not easy. David and Japhet had to wait until the swell raised them to the level of a rocky platform so that they could leap out to hold the boat. While they were trying to judge the right moment to jump, Peregrine flew inland, where he found a wandering albatross perched on the flax-thatched roof of one of the small, sturdy cottages.

Strangers were rare on the island, so the albatross was happy to give directions as to where Peregrine would find his plant. He looked forward to settling down for a long talk with this bird with the odd interest in botany. But Peregrine had no time for more than the barest politeness before he flew up to the crater edge of the island's volcano and plucked a root and branch of the silver-gray plant growing there. He hoped the albatross knew a dragonbane from a sparrow grass.

Rhiannon nodded when she saw the fernlike leaves.

"Yes, that is how the Sibyl described it to me. Come, let us make haste to Iceland before it is too late."

She touched the magic runes again, and the coracle turned north. David and Japhet strained their eyes for a last look at Tristan da Cunha. They thought how nice it would have been to poke around a little, and perhaps collect a new song or two, but didn't say that aloud, since they knew how urgent it was to waste no time in returning to Caradoc's aid. The albatross followed them for a little way, still hoping for a good chat, but the coracle soon became a speck on the horizon. So he flapped back to his watching post, where nothing ever happened, wondering about the rush.

As soon as the coast of Iceland came into sight, Peregrine took the dragonbane in his beak and flew to find the Wise Woman at a speed he had seldom achieved in his old days hunting for Prince Math. When he finally brought the completed spell to Caradoc on the Vatnajökull glacier, he was not a moment too soon. The flames of Caradoc's enemy had cut through mists, melt waters, and other defenses and were now beginning to scorch and darken the dragon's bronze scales.

The dragonbane must have changed, or the Sibyl's memory been at fault. The dragon's fire did not go out. Instead, the ground cracked open at his feet, and he plummeted down into the earth. The crevasse closed again, and the Korean dragon was imprisoned deep under the land of Iceland. There, none of his struggles could free him, and whenever he thought of Caradoc he became so infuriated that he would spit flames, and at the surface his fire would erupt in a volcano. His everyday fury was enough to heat water deep underground, which bubbled up in warm geysers.

"Warm water outside my door is a comfort I had not looked for," said the Sibyl, "although I had heard that you are good at providing it.

"Take my boat for your own. Saint Bride herself gave it to me a lifetime ago. I foresee you will use it well."

Then the Companions lightly touched the magic runes, and their stone coracle sped, straight as an arrow, for Wales.

"No," said Caradoc firmly, "that was no good deed. That was self-defense. In truth, it was very nearly the end of the last Welsh dragon. If you hadn't saved me with the dragonbane, it is I, and not the Korean nuisance, who would currently be the foundation of Iceland's heating system."

"What is round and stone and sails to Tristan da Cunha?" asked Japhet, who loved riddles. "That is surely good for a song, David?"

David reached eagerly for his harp, but Rhiannon interrupted to say, "Epics sung by musical lambs about the North and South Atlantic are all very well, but Caradoc, do not lose sight of the fact that we still have business to attend to nearer home, if home it is to be."

the golden bird

THE COMPANIONS were brewing elderflower tea to celebrate finishing Caradoc's new herb garden when Peregrine pointed out a strange boat coming in to Caernarfon harbor. In the center of its single buff sail was a curious symbol, of three legs endlessly running round in a circle. They watched the boat tie up at the quay and saw a small procession come ashore and wind its way up the hillside toward them.

The strangers bowed very low, and ceremoniously presented a gift to Caradoc. It was a marvelous chess set, carved of walrus ivory. As Caradoc set it out, the Companions gazed in awe at the knights on snorting horses, the large-eyed queens lost in thought, and the stern kings, each with a sword across his knees. Even the pawns were intricately carved with never-ending whorls and spirals. The hair on Japhet's neck prickled at the sheer beauty of the wonderful pieces.

"Why does the King of the Isle of Man send me such a treasure?" asked Caradoc, who had recognized the three-legged symbol.

"Lord," was the reply, "he sends you his second most precious possession because his Wise Women have told him that only you can help him regain his first and greatest treasure, his daughter."

Caradoc invited them to drink his elderflower tea. They did so, bravely, as they told their story.

"Lords," said their spokesman, "you know that the Isle of Man is not large, nor is it rich, but we are free men there. Our king is the first among equals, and we all meet in the Tynwald parliament each year, to decide the laws that govern our country."

He took a sip of the pale yellow tea and hastily added as much honey as the beaker would hold.

"Now, the Kings of Cumbria," he continued, "have long coveted our island. For many generations they have failed to capture it in war or win it in peace, until they have come to feel that it is the one place on earth they must own.

"This year they assembled a great war fleet and sailed over on the spring tide. Before we were awake they had entered the palace and captured our princess." He choked; whether from emotion or from Caradoc's dreadful brew was not clear. His friends finished the tale:

"The princess is held captive on the mainland. They have refused all our offers of a ransom. Now we hear that on her tenth birthday she will be married to the King of Cumbria, who will then claim the Isle of Man for himself."

The Manxmen all looked more and more dismal as this bad news was unfolded. So did Caradoc. He could see clearly the calamity threatening the princess and the whole island. The King of Cumbria was older than Princess Angharad's own father; furthermore, he was known far and wide as a mean and brutal despot. The Cumbrian's first business would be to crush Manx independence by dismissing the parliament. Then he would doubtless go on to obliterate the Manx language, the people's customs, and their laws.

"Will you come?" pleaded the Manxmen.

"Tonight," said Caradoc, who had been lectured the night before by Rhiannon on doing his good deeds no farther than a score of wingbeats from his own hearth. "It is barely a flame-throw to the Isle of Man," he assured her.

"Only if your geography is as weak as Japhet's," said she, not fooled.

When his watchers reported the return of the boat from Wales, the King of Man hastened down to the harbor to greet his emissaries.

"I am not hopeful," he said somberly.

"She is our only child," grieved the queen.

"I think," murmured Rhiannon, "you should send us to the Cumbrian court as your special envoys, to see matters for ourselves."

"Speak up, bird," said the king, and when Rhiannon's suggestion was repeated to him, he agreed. "Of course. Excellent idea! Take my ring. Ten strong members of the Tynwald will sail you there themselves."

"Thank you," said Caradoc politely. "We realize the honor, but our stone coracle is quicker."

"Just as you like," replied the king, giving up any hope that this strange Welsh group could aid him.

Hopeless was a mild word for the way things looked in Cumbria. When the Companions presented the ring, the king had some sharp words to say about the strange creatures the King of Man thought fit to send as ambassadors. He refused to let them see Princess Angharad, who was trying hard to be brave in her cold and lonely prison. Peregrine, after flying over the castle keep where the princess was guarded, reported that there was no way in which even the bravest and most determined band of Manxmen could rescue the girl.

"Exactly what I found, chatting to the guard hounds," confirmed Japhet. "This good deed will take some doing."

"All the more reason for doing it," said Peregrine, who was at his bravest when things looked impossible.

That night the king and his court dined well, but not wisely. Full of wine and pride, the king dismissed the Companions.

"Go back and tell the King of the Isle of Man that since his daughter is said to be as good as gold, I will send her back only in return for her weight in that metal." The Cumbrian king laughed heartily at his own joke, and his courtiers laughed after him. It was well known that there was no gold in the Isle of Man.

Caradoc replied, "Sire, what message is that? The Manxmen are poor and could not find a sparrow's weight in gold."

The king laughed even louder and said, "Don't I know it? I can't think why I want their miserable island, except that I fancy that title 'King of Man.' The poor fools could not find one feather's weight of gold to ransom their princess." The court all laughed obediently at the wit and wisdom of their king.

"Even so, Your Majesty would never dare make such an offer," put in Rhiannon swiftly. She knew the King of Cumbria prided himself on his boldness.

"Would not dare?" roared the king. "Who uses such words to the most daring man in the West? Of course I dare," he bellowed and, striking his hand on the table, said, "If the people of Man can send me an exact featherweight of gold before the princess's tenth birthday, they shall have their brat back."

All the Cumbrian courtiers applauded the joke. "Our clever king," they told one another. "Our wily ruler." They all knew that, even in the unlikely event of some gold being found, there could be endless argument as to whether a featherweight was measured by the down of an eider duck or by an eagle's pinion. The talking on that alone would comfortably take them past any tenth birthday, or twentieth, for that matter. But Rhiannon was content.

There was a glum silence on the return to the Isle of Man. David broke it by saying flatly, "We cannot possibly hope to find enough gold within the time."

"Besides," said Peregrine, equally despondent, "think of the months they will spend disputing the kind of feather intended."

"Poor, poor Angharad," whispered soft-hearted Japhet.

Rhiannon was heard to murmur sleepily that she had sent her a message of cheer by a mouse. Rhiannon, the owl, had ways of convincing mice.

"Whatever can we do?" wailed David, wondering if he knew enough verses of a suitable lament to play for the royal parents.

Rhiannon opened one bright eye and said, very

distinctly, "My friends, we are going to find the Bird of the Golden West."

The stone coracle sailed north, through rain and cloud and waves and wind. Only Caradoc was cheerful, remembering the old days on the Irish coast. Everyone else was cold and bedraggled.

Whenever they stopped among the isles of the Inner and Outer Hebrides no one could tell them where the Golden Bird might be. Until, at last, beyond the westernmost isle, they saw a thicker mist, and Caradoc, who knew something about mysteries in mists, sailed straight for it. They felt the keel grate and then ground, and found themselves at the foot of a mighty cliff.

At the top a great golden bird looked fixedly out to sea, as though they did not exist.

"Beautiful Bird of the Golden West," began Rhiannon. The bird did not blink a golden eyelid.

"Honorable Golden Bird," tried Caradoc. The bird stared straight at the western horizon.

"Lady Bird," started David, but somehow it didn't sound right.

"Fellow Bird," said Peregrine hopefully. No answer.

"Pretty birdie," murmured Japhet, and got a reproving glare from Caradoc.

There seemed nothing for it but to tell their story, make their request, and hope for a reply.

When the story was done, there was a long silence. Then, just as the watery sun was slipping below the horizon, the Golden Bird spoke. In a barely intelligible croak, she asked, "What is Angharad to me or I to her that I should painfully pluck out my feathers for her?"

Then there was another long silence while the Golden Bird looked morosely into the darkening west, and the Companions tried, and failed, to think of something to say.

David and Japhet remembered that they were wet, hungry, and tired. Caradoc cheered them somewhat by blowing a fire. Peregrine further improved matters by catching enough fish for supper, so at least they did not have to eat the cold seaweed salad Japhet had feared. Afterwards, to ward off the low spirits that were threatening to set in, David played his harp.

Rhiannon glanced through the dark and saw that the Golden Bird was not looking quite as directly west. David played on. Rhiannon asked Caradoc to tell them how it felt to be the last dragon in the Western World. Caradoc talked, as he seldom did, of being different from everyone else and of wishing that, just once, he could talk to another dragon. He spoke of his regret at having had to imprison one of the last of his kind, the Korean dragon, deep under the ice of Iceland. And wondered, ruefully, if he had tried hard enough to make his old enemy see that fire was better used for warming than for war.

The bird moved its head a fraction more, and Rhiannon could see in the moonlight a great, golden tear welling up in its mournful eye. Its rarely used voice came creaking from the cliff edge: "You are a novice in loneliness. Wait until you have lived three hundred years without seeing one of your own kind."

There was another long silence.

Japhet, who had lived in so many places that home for him was not the dimly remembered, rock-strewn slopes of far Mount Ararat, but wherever the people he loved were, said, "Perhaps the best deed of all would be for us to come and live here to cheer up that doleful bird. We can always do it if the Welsh drive us out," he added, blithely unconscious of the number of claws on which he was stepping.

Rhiannon remarked in more heartfelt tones than she usually allowed herself, "I trust it will not come to that. An occasional Welsh mist is one thing, but this perpetual Scottish fog is quite another matter."

At last they went to sleep, thinking of mists, loneliness, gold feathers, ruthless kings, and whether St. MacDara could possibly convert an angry Korean dragon. Dreaming unhappily of such things, they missed the soft flap of golden wing-beats.

Daylight next morning showed the bird had gone. The Companions trailed down to their boat, thinking of the captive princess and of how they could possibly tell her father of their failure. Peregrine flew up to his usual perch, and there, at the top of the mast, gleamed a single golden feather. Something had melted the Golden Bird's frozen heart. She had left them their answer to the King of Cumbria: the ransom for Angharad.

All of Caradoc's sailing skill and the magic of the runes went into making the coracle skim swiftly south once more.

When the King of Cumbria heard that the Manx ambassadors had returned and wished to see him, he was irritated.

"How many times do I have to see those peculiarities the King of Man sends over as envoys? Once is enough. Once can be amusing, but I hate to do anything twice."

Then he cheered up, as he thought of the humiliation he was about to inflict on them.

"I don't doubt they have sold that scrap of an emerald in the royal Manx ring for gold. It will probably weigh as a wren's feather. I will demand the weight of a goose feather."

"Lord, do you mean a wing feather or a breast feather?" asked a daring noble.

"Idiot, numbskull, cretin!" stormed the king. "Are you so dim that you cannot see that is just the catch? The Manxmen can never get it right."

"Alas, that I am not as wise as my king," said the noble quickly.

"Fill the Great Hall," ordered the king. "Bring Princess Angharad. I want every person at court to witness my defeat of the ambassadors from Man. If only they had sent ones more worthy of me. The bards shall compose a song in honor of my wit.

Everyone is to remember this day when I am King of Man.

"King of Man," he repeated, rolling it round his tongue.

"We are going to find that song tedious after the hundredth repetition," muttered one noble to another, safely at the back of the Hall.

The Great Hall filled. Angharad was brought to stand near the scales, which were to weigh the gold against a feather. The court kitchens had supplied feathers of ducks, pigeons, and blackbirds. Two pages brought in a rook feather, a missel-thrush feather, and the red feather from a robin's breast; all different sizes and weights. The chamberlain held them in readiness and stifled a sneeze, as the king beckoned Caradoc to come forward.

"Put your gold in the scales, my good — er — reptile. We will determine whether it is indeed a featherweight, no more and no less."

"Lord, that is not necessary," replied Caradoc. "I have here a golden feather. Not a feather's weight

of gold, but a feather that is itself gold. You will agree that is the exact ransom you demanded for the princess."

The fury and chagrin of the king were such that David half expected him to explode with wrath on the spot. He watched the royal tantrum with interest, but not for long. Caradoc prudently whisked his companions and the princess away while the king was still bellowing about treason, trickery, and troublesome beasts. In the uproar and confusion of the court, their exit went unnoticed, until too late.

On the Isle of Man, the rejoicing did not stop for a week. The king and queen begged the Companions to stay and to consider themselves honorary members of the Tynwald and Manx beasts extraordinary. Caradoc declined the honor and, to take the sting out of the refusal, explained his need to earn the right to remain in North Wales. The king nodded. The queen protested, "Gwynedd is pretty enough, and I have no doubt you are attached to your own cave, but I always think no place can equal the Isle of Man. Do come and make your home here instead of in Wales. We would set you no tests."

Caradoc smiled, the rare dragon smile, and said, "Madam, your own words have explained why you must live in the Isle of Man and I must live in Wales."

So at the end of the week of celebrations, the Companions said farewell, launched the coracle, and sailed for Wales, for a certain cave and a chess tournament that lasted a month.

"I have been thinking about the dragon loneliness I mentioned to the Golden Bird," said Caradoc in the glow of pleasure that came from checkmating Peregrine's king, "and I have just realized that I have not felt it this last half-year, my friends."

THE FLOATING ISLAND

I N LATE JUNE the cuckoo sang its bubbling farewells. The curlews called to each other across
the moorland, where they had made their nest.
The plovers and skylarks made the hillside sweet
with their twittering, and on rare evenings the
Companions even heard the heart-melting sounds
of the singing birds of Queen Rhiannon.

All this music revived David's half-forgotten
purpose of becoming a wandering bard. But wandering no longer seemed as attractive as it had
when he was lonely and homeless. So he played a
little for his friends one night and announced,
"What I really need are some more lessons from
my old teacher, David of the White Rock."

"A good idea," said Caradoc, perhaps a little more promptly than was polite. "We would accompany you, but I still must prove myself to the people of Caernarfon."

So David set off south alone, following the curve of Cardigan Bay. Until he arrived in Llanarth, he was rather pleased with the welcome he got in each village, where he played his harp in return for his supper.

In Llanarth, things were very different. No one smiled at the sight of a black lamb with a harp. When he played his merry tunes, they looked sad, and his sad tunes made the villagers nod their heads in agreement.

Finally, instead of telling stories himself, David asked the people gathered to hear him why they were so miserable. And so he heard about the sorrows of Llanarth.

Three years ago, he was told, Viking raiders, prowling along the coast, had caught sight of the snug little haven. They landed and, finding the people had fled, plundered their homes, stole their goods, killed their pigs and chickens, and finally overturned the great Cross at which St. Non herself had spoken. Mabon, their Man of God, had lost his life bravely trying to protect his church. The church itself was set ablaze, and their one great possession, the gold cup St. Patrick had brought

74

them from Ireland when he came to dedicate their church, was lost.

When the Vikings left, the people doused the flames, rebuilt their homes, and mourned their priest. But since that dreadful night, nothing had gone well. Children had died of fevers. The oat crop had been blighted two summers in succession. The cows gave little milk, and the ewes had no lambs. Worst of all, as David could see clearly, the villagers had given up hope and were resigned to expecting the very worst to happen in a dismal future.

The sadness was catching. Next day David went miserably on his way. The blue of Cardigan Bay seemed too cheerful now, so he picked his way inland and up the gray granite sides of the Preseli Hills, thinking them to be more in tune with his somber mood.

At midday he stopped to rest by a lake with an island in it, an island that seemed both near and distant, and all the time particularly enticing. A kestrel hawk hovered, almost motionless, overhead. Then, with deadly accuracy, it fell out of the sky and rose heavily, carrying something small and black in its talons. While David watched, the little captive wriggled free and fell into the lake. The commotion and frantic squeaks that reached him sent David straight into the water, trusting the air trapped under his curly wool to hold him

up. Breathlessly, he reached the waterlogged mole, coming up for its last gasp. It twisted its paws in David's coat, and together they reached the island, panting but safe.

The mole dived into a burrow, and David looked around the island. In the middle grew a gnarled apple tree, from which hung some unripe, golden fruit. But what interested him far more was the mat of strawberry plants underfoot. Hunting carefully through it, David found just three late berries. They were quite the most delectable-looking fruit he had ever seen, and he popped one into his mouth.

The taste was all you ever dreamed a strawberry could be. When David finished licking the last traces of it from his lips, he heard a multitude of voices and looked around for their owners. The island seemed empty and alone in the lake, but his newly acute hearing could make out one high, excited voice in particular, explaining its escape from death by land, air, and water. It could only be the mole.

David put his mouth to the burrow and inquired, "Anybody at home?"

A mole popped out and said, "Oh, you found a strawberry, did you? I thought they were all gone."

Then she said, "Thank you most kindly for saving Moldywarp ap Woof. What can we do for you in return?"

"Please explain why I can hear so many different voices," said David. "I think I can hear everyone in Wales speaking at once."

"You can," said the mole, and she explained that they were on the Floating Island of the Blessed Brân, and that anyone who ate the fruit of that island had the gift of such acute hearing that there was no talk in the whole land that they could not listen to if they so wished.

"Many people have spent a lifetime seeking it," she added.

David thought he caught Caradoc's rumble in Caernarfon and hastily began to hum so as not to eavesdrop. He stowed the other two berries carefully behind his ears, being short of pockets, and wondered whether his new hearing was really such a blessing, as he looked around for some moss to make earplugs.

"Don't worry," said the mole; "it doesn't last long. Now," she continued briskly, "if you have nothing in mind, my people have a gift they would like to give you in return for saving our dear Moldy."

To David's polite disclaimers the mole said, "Actually, my dear lamb, the gift we have in mind is a dreadful nuisance to us. You would be doing us all a good turn by accepting it."

Being a helpful sort of lamb, David did as the mole asked and, guided by an odd assortment of squeaking moles, chattering voles, chirruping grasshoppers, squawking bugs, and even whispering earthworms, reached a large molehill, where his new friends were heaving up a grubby object.

"Ruins our western advances," they grumbled. "Glad to give it to you."

David took it gingerly, washed off the dirt in the lake, and found himself holding a small, rough, golden cup, all twined with the never-ending symbols of eternity. He knew what it must be at once and wished he could shout the good news all the way to Llanarth, where he could hear the villagers talking:

"Bad day, Mrs. Pugh."

"Shocking, isn't it, Mrs. Jones? But then they're all alike nowadays. Not a good one among them."

"Wait till you see what I've got!" cried David. But of course they couldn't hear him.

He waved a hasty hoof at his new friends and plunged into the lake again. Once he had reached the shore, he didn't stop running until he reached the Cross of St. Non in the middle of Llanarth.

The villagers were overjoyed. They smiled smiles that had not been used in three years, feeling that this amazing reappearance of their treasure was a sign of the return of good fortune. They begged David to stay on, make his home with them, and help in the building of a new church.

David refused the honor of being their lucky lamb, saying his friend Caradoc needed one of those around, but he explained how he had found the cup. It was clear that the priest had had no time to tell anybody where he had buried the treasure for safekeeping.

Before he left, David gave his second strawberry to the townspeople of Llanarth so that they could hear the moles telling what else had been hidden

underground from the Vikings and lost when the owners did not live to tell the secret.

The third strawberry he gave to David of the White Rock, who listened to the sound of the whole land: to the meaning of the swallows' song, the otters' laugh, and the badgers' chortle. He made more wonderful music from his new understanding than anyone had dreamed possible.

"Thank you," said Caradoc gently to an eager lamb back in North Wales. "A most generous offer, but I don't think it can be counted on my tally of good deeds when it was all yours. However, I would dearly love to visit the island you speak of."

"Make up a song about it," suggested Peregrine, promptly flying out of earshot.

"What floats on water and is sometimes eaten for breakfast?" tried Japhet. "The Blessed Brân, of course."

Whenever they pass through the Preseli Hills, the Companions always look for the Floating Island of the Blessed Brân. But even Peregrine's and Rhiannon's sharp eyes have never spotted it again.

FINN OF THE FIFTY FIGHTS

I N THE SINGLE sunny interval of a wet July week, the Companions thankfully left the shelter of the cave. Outside, Japhet practiced bouncing a gooseberry on his nose, until it finally burst. Then he began to teach David how to roll an accurate marble. Rhiannon cast an amused eye on a line of young swallows reluctant to try flying. Caradoc went on muttering, as he had for the past seven days, "I really must go and see the Weather Book at Glastonbury. There has to be some way to mend the matter of this misbegotten Welsh weather. That might be the best deed of all."

Peregrine was watching a small black dot, invisible to the others, pull past Bardsey Island and make its way laboriously along the coast.

"I think I will go and see exactly what that is," he said and took off.

Some hours later Peregrine returned with a tired, worried, wave-soaked Irish monk, who was grateful for a warm welcome and Caradoc's fire at which to dry himself.

"Between me and my God, a hard coming I had of it. Sailing a curragh across the Irish Sea is weary work in the best of seasons, and ye'll not deny that this is the worst of summers."

Steam rose from the monk's woollen tunic as it dried, and he began to look almost cheerful at the sight of a bubbling pot of broth and the smell of a browning leek-and-potato pie. But he was a man in the habit of being strict with himself and putting duty before desires of the flesh. So, despite his hunger, he would not eat before telling the Companions what mission had brought him across the sea to find them.

"There is woe in all Ireland," began the monk in an arresting fashion. "The great Book of Kells itself has vanished. No hide nor hair of it can we find, though we have looked high and low, far and near. 'Twas the saint, the blessed MacDara himself, who sent me to seek your help, for we are at our wit's end."

"What is the Book of Kells?" Japhet asked Rhiannon.

He asked very quietly, for fear of being thought a know-nothing, but Caradoc overheard him.

"It is a copy of the Gospels and one of the greatest treasures of the Celtic world," he answered kindly. "When Saint Columba built his church at Kells, many of the best artists and most learned people in Ireland went to live there. Between them, they decorated the Holy Book as richly as they knew how. It has grand lettering, and each page is surrounded with pictures and patterns all in bright colors and pure gold. The book is famed far and wide for its beauty. I saw it myself once, when Saint MacDara and I made the journey to Kells." Caradoc paused and went on slowly, "It was the most beautiful book I could ever hope to see in my lifetime."

Japhet did know some things. He knew, for instance, that a dragon's lifetime is a very long matter indeed. The Book of Kells must be a true marvel.

"The blue and gold of the capital letters," remembered Caradoc, "and the way in which they would curve and flow, and weave in and out of an entire page, turned my insides to water with their sheer loveliness."

"A fortunate reaction, considering what a fire hazard you were," said Rhiannon tartly. "By the way, I hope you are not considering going to Ireland. There is a matter of half a dozen good deeds or so to be done here first."

Caradoc puffed an affectionate smoke ring at her and then turned back to the monk.

"Surely only Viking raiders would be so bold and so reckless as to steal the Holy Book, which is the pride of Ireland?"

"There have been no Viking raids anywhere in the country for a twelvemonth, God be praised," the holy man replied.

"You must have some other clues?"

"Before God, there are no clues," the monk said.

He stopped talking while he ate enough leek-and-potato pie for ten. Japhet watched a little glumly as all hopes of a second helping vanished. After supper, the holy man turned to Caradoc again and said, "Saint MacDara insisted that I tell you the tale of the humiliation of Finn of the Fifty Fights, although, God knows, it has little enough to do with the grievous loss of the Book of Kells."

The Companions loved stories. They settled more comfortably around the fire while the monk told them about Finn, with his fiery red hair and flaming temper to match, who was proudest of all the proud chieftains of Ireland. Finn ruled over Galway. It was the poorest and smallest province in the Kingdom of Connaught, and that might have had something to do with his quickness to see an insult where none was intended.

On All Saints' Day, after the harvest was in, the chieftains of Ireland met at the palace of the High King in Tara, as they did every year. Finn of the Fifty Fights was there, bristling with fury because his clothes were the shabbiest and his sword the most battered of any in Tara. When he was asked to take the lowest place at the table, as was fitting for the ruler of the smallest province, his rage boiled over. Kicking over the seat, he stormed out of the gathering. Unfortunately, Finn failed, in his rage, to remember the door's low lintel and his own great height. He bumped his skull with a crack that sounded round the Hall and sent him tumbling head over heels. The whole company burst out laughing, while Finn picked himself up in a black cloud of dust and fury. Straightway he departed for Galway, swearing that he would not rest until he had avenged himself on the laughers for their insult.

"What did he do?" asked David, thinking this was just the stuff for a bard.

"Nothing has been heard of him since. He must be still simmering in his castle in Galway. Pray God he does not boil over again, one day," added the monk.

Early next morning the Companions went down to the secret place, where once the boats from Rome had landed with supplies for the Legions at the forgotten port of Segontium. There they launched

85

the stone coracle from its hiding place. Rhiannon touched the magic runes, despite some resigned owl mutterings about travel being against her better judgment, and they sped lightly across the Irish Sea. The monk marveled all the way at the ease with which he returned, compared with his hardships in coming to Wales.

"Ye'll be going to Kells," he assumed, as they landed at the foot of the Giant's Causeway.

"No," replied Caradoc, "Galway seems as good a place to start our search as any. Saint MacDara will have had his reasons for asking you to tell us of the fury of Finn."

They bade the holy man good-bye, and sailed on westward.

The castle of Finn of the Fifty Fights turned out to be rather a ramshackle affair of earthworks, mounds, ditches, wooden towers, dormitories, and workshops. There was such coming and going in the central courtyard that the arrival of another group, however unlikely, attracted little attention.

"Ye'll be the entertainers for the feast," said the gatekeeper. "'Tis a week early, but ye're welcome. We could do with some entertainment, with himself in the sulks all year."

The Companions set to work.

By night they entertained the company that col-

86

lected around the fire in the courtyard when the day's work was done. Japhet, who loved an audience, juggled hard-boiled eggs and onions with energy, if not total accuracy. David made the most of his chance, at last, to be a wandering minstrel. Peregrine did a nice line in skydiving and aerial somersaults. But every evening the grand climax of their performance was Caradoc's flame-throwing and fire-swallowing display.

By day, unnoticed in the rush and bustle of preparations, they searched the castle up and down, through and through, from motte to bailey, and back again. Rhiannon slipped silently in and out of shadows and windows. Peregrine strained his keen eyes to the utmost. Caradoc rumbled round and round, causing considerable comment in the countryside. David and Japhet eagerly poked their noses into things that did not concern them. Not one of them, however, caught a glimpse of the stolen treasure or even heard so much as a rumor as to its whereabouts.

"That book certainly isn't here, or we should have found it by now. We should move on to Ulster," suggested David.

"Perhaps we should ask the advice of the Singing Swans," wondered Rhiannon.

"Now, wait!" yelped Japhet in dismay. He had been chatting in the kitchens all day. "We can't possibly leave before the feast. They say that Finn means to make it one that people will tell their grandchildren about. So how can I tell mine, one day, that I wasn't there? That we left the night before it began?"

"Then we will stay for the feast," decided Caradoc, who had not missed noticing some signs of preparations for war. He was also curious as to what Finn intended to say to his captains. "But as soon as it is over we must continue our search elsewhere. After all, we have come to Ireland to find the Book of Kells."

Now, Finn of the Fifty Fights was anxious for the Captains of Galway to fall in with his plans for avenging the insult paid him at Tara. He intended no less than to go to war and overthrow the High King, but he was shrewd enough to know that it would be extremely difficult to persuade the captains to follow him on so rash an enterprise. So he had arranged a little drama to impress them. But first, he intended to flatter them with a feast such as they had never seen. His lands had been scoured for wild boars, venison, geese, capons, salmon and eels, even herons and blackbirds. His kitchens had worked nonstop to stew and stuff and roast and baste. They were making swans out of butter from every cow in Galway. There were pounds of syllabub, lakes of gooseberry fool, and puddings and pies galore.

In the Great Hall, at last, the knife went into the

meat and the drink into the horn. The mead flowed from vast barrels all evening. Finally Finn felt mellow, for the first time since Tara, and boasted, with an oath, that the day was coming when the tables would be reversed and the Chieftain of Galway would no longer be given the lowliest place.

"I swear that ye shall not see the sun rise on next All Saints' Day unless ye also see Finn of the Fifty Fights sitting in the place of honor, at the head of the table. The country's greatest treasure shall be under my right hand, and all Ireland shall do me honor as High King in Tara."

At these words, the Companions pricked up their respective wool, hair, feathers, and scales.

After the feast there were the usual storytellers, bards, tumblers, and jugglers. Peregrine, with difficulty, persuaded Japhet not to join the latter, in case his ability to drop balls would betray them all, now that the real entertainers were there.

Toward midnight, there was a commotion at the end of the Hall, and three aged crones entered. Finn looked surprised. But Rhiannon, who was skilled at reading faces, thought the look poorly covered a mood of impatience that the three had taken so long to appear.

The company stared, mesmerized, as the three sisters hobbled over to the fire, threw onto it three handfuls of damp elder twigs, and turned to face the king. With the smoke curling around them in

fine theatrical fashion, they chanted, one after the other:

"All hail Finn of Galway."

"All hail Lord of Connaught."

"All hail Destiny of Ireland."

The first crone poked the fire with her stick so that the elder wood and peat blazed up briefly.

"The Fates send a message."

"A message for him of the Fifty Fights."

"A sign for all Galway."

The second crone threw a handful of dry bracken onto the dying flames so that they spurted up again.

"If you would read the sign, seek amid the Standing Stones."

"If you would obey the Fates, search the Place of the Menhirs."

"If you would learn the future, look among the Old Ones."

Then, all together, in a discordant chant that made David wince, they said, "A great Irish treasure lies hidden. He who finds it is worthy of becoming High King in Tara."

The bracken flames guttered out. Their singsong over, the crones disappeared. A great hubbub broke out in the Hall. Rhiannon watched Finn try to hide his satisfaction at the way his little plan had gone.

"By my red beard," he said, "this is most strange. We must find out for ourselves what secret the menhirs hold."

Peregrine wondered where the visitors had come from and where they were going. He went to see what he could see and was rewarded by the sight of three old women hopping nimbly onto three ponies, whose new saddlebags were being stuffed to bursting by Finn's own servant.

Hours later, when everyone was at last asleep, the Companions, guided by starlight, the odd puff of flame from Caradoc, and Rhiannon's useful ability to see in the dark, made their cautious way up to the great circle of Standing Stones above Galway Bay. A thorn tree, misshapen by winds from the Atlantic, had taken root near the center. Rhiannon peered intently around the space inside the circle and then pointed out some uneven ground at the foot of the tree. "I wonder who-oo has been making those mounds?"

Japhet set to work with a will, and dug among the roots with breathless speed, while Caradoc gave him light and moved out of his way the pile of dirt he was making.

David kept trying to give good advice. "Gently does it. Left paw down a bit. Would it help if I sang you a digging song?"

To which Japhet, concentrating on the work at hand, could say only, "Arf!"

"Half?" said the lamb, puzzled. "You only want half a song?"

Japhet struck something hard, and they all leaned over to see what it might be. It turned out to be a small coffer of bog oak. Inside the coffer was the very book they sought—the book that Finn had stolen in his scheme for revenge. Caradoc gently breathed some more fire, and by its light the Companions gasped at the beauty of the marvelous pages of the Book of Kells.

Tearing his eyes away from it with difficulty, Peregrine said, "The straightest way is the safest way. I will fly to Kells this very night with the treasure." David unslung his harp, which he never willingly let out of his sight, and sacrificed three of its strings with only the faintest of sighs. Rhiannon knotted them tight, and Peregrine rose into the air, closely grasping the strings, which formed

a sort of cat's cradle around the book. The considerable weight was lightened by the thought of the joy with which he would be greeted at Kells.

Meanwhile, Caradoc, having placed a parchment of his own inside the bog-oak coffer, was carefully replacing it in its hiding place under the thorn tree.

"Well," he said with satisfaction as he finished tamping the turf into position, "perhaps the Fates will have a different message for the Captains of Galway from the one Finn expects."

Japhet shivered a little in the shadow of the ancient menhirs and was glad to return to the castle's untidy courtyard.

All the next day the castle resounded with the jingle of harness and the clatter of weapons, as fighting men from all corners of Galway arrived. After the feast, Finn of the Fifty Fights had sent runners around the kingdom, summoning them all to the Place of the Menhirs.

When the great force was assembled on the headland above Galway Bay, where the Standing Stones had stood in their mysterious circle for hundreds of years, Finn strode to the center and, with one hand on the great capstone, said:

"Brave men of Galway, you have heard how the three Wise Women have foretold that in this place a sign will be found to change the history of Ireland. Now, this very night I have dreamed that the menhirs will tell us that the war I propose will be crowned with success, and that my destiny is to rule over Ireland and be lord of all its treasures."

He instructed the four Wardens of Galway to dig in four places within the stone circle. When one of them struck the coffer beneath the thorn tree, Finn said, "Open, my lord, and tell us all what message the menhirs have sent."

He leaned his chin on his hand, the better to disguise the look of satisfaction that he could not keep from spreading over his face. The bog-oak coffer was opened, the parchment unrolled. In a loud, clear voice the warden read to the entire multitude:

"Go to war and you will destroy the fair Kingdom of Galway."

Finn of the Fifty Fights jumped as if a swarm of bees had stung him. In vain he raged, entreated, explained. His army disbanded that very night. Not a captain was left in Castle Finn. In his rage and misery, Finn shut himself up on an island in the remote Lake of Innisfree. For a year and a day, nobody so much as clapped eyes on him, while he ate nothing but beans and ground his teeth as he thought of the glory that had been so nearly within his grasp.

Back in Wales, the Companions feasted in sticky satisfaction on the Irish heather honey and bannock cakes with which the grateful monks had loaded their coracle to the sinking point, and they looked with pride at the illuminated message of appreciation that had been inscribed for them by the entire community at Kells.

"Noses to the grindstone," said Japhet. "A good deed a day from now on. The town fathers turned down my suggestion for a riddle-composing course, so I shall go and teach the children of Caernarfon how to roll marbles."

"I will teach them music," said David, getting up eagerly.

Caradoc was moved. He was well aware that the dog and the lamb were welcome to stay in Gwynedd. It was only the dragon who was on trial.

ᴄhe ᴄhin man

O NE BRISK August morning the Companions
were sitting outside their cave, watching
the gulls wheel and swoop over the Menai
Straits. Although it was still summer, Caradoc had
shivered under his scales all morning. So he made
a fire, which now gave a comfortable heat to their
backs.

The smell of food sizzling was just getting to a
particularly agreeable stage, when up the hill toward them came the thinnest man they had ever
seen. He was more skinny than a squirrel in spring.
His cheeks were hollow. His skin hung in wrinkles
like an elderly apple. There was so little flesh at the
end of his nose that two small bones showed white

96

under the skin. David and Japhet both secretly rubbed their own noses, feeling, thankfully, that they were as round as ever. The thin man's clothes sagged about him in droops and folds that suggested he had once been a fatter man, although now he made a beanpole look stout.

Caradoc saw that the stranger's eyes were fixed on the food. So he hastily blew up the fire, finished the potatoes he was frying, and offered them to the visitor. The thin man promptly sat down on a bony bottom, and ate and ate and ate.

"You would think he had not seen food for a month," said Japhet to Peregrine, as he watched the pile of potatoes Caradoc had intended for the five of them disappear. "I only wish Caradoc had been frying those endless parsnips when he walked up."

The thin man ate his way through the potatoes, six kippers, a bowl of oatmeal, two dozen welshcakes, and a loaf of speckled bread.

David and Japhet were impressed.

Rhiannon sent both of them out to see what else was available in the garden. They found some beans ready to pick, several stalks of rhubarb, and added a bunch of parsley, sage, rosemary, and thyme for good measure. Returning with this interesting mixture, they found they were just in time to hear the stranger begin his story.

"I come from Caerphilly Castle, from the household of Thomas ap Thomas, Lord of Morgannwg, where a great misfortune has befallen us, so that everyone is twice as lean and hungry as I am."

"He is joking," said Japhet, luckily quietly enough not to be heard by their visitor, who went on, absently munching a stalk of rhubarb:

"On Midsummer Day it is the custom of Thomas ap Thomas to hold a feast in his castle. This year we sat down to eat at overflowing tables. The kitchens had provided food enough for an entire year."

He paused dramatically. The Companions leaned forward to hear what came next.

"But not so much as a crumb of it did we taste."

"Why not?" asked Peregrine. He was always direct.

"Because straightway everyone in the Hall fell fast asleep. When we awoke, the food was gone and we were still hungry. From that day to this, no sooner do we sit down to eat than we fall asleep, and the meal disappears. It is the same in every house in the town. Our best efforts have failed to discover what enemy is so persecuting us. Now our storehouses are empty, and as the strongest of our people, I was chosen to go and seek supplies from the men of Môn, who have the best-stocked barns in all of Wales. On the island of Môn, they said that I needed your help more than I needed sacks of oats and barley. They sent me here. Good lords, I pray you, come and undo the spell that is upon us."

The thin man fumbled awkwardly in a pouch for some of the gold he had brought to pay the farmers of Môn, not sure if you were required to pay an agreeable dragon in gold.

"No, keep your money," said Caradoc. "You may yet need to buy barley meal."

The notion that the Jack Sprat in front of them was the stoutest person to be found in all the household of Thomas ap Thomas was enough to persuade the Companions to return with him at once.

"It won't take long," Caradoc reassured Rhiannon, "and we have the whole autumn in front of us. Plenty of time to satisfy the good people of Caernarfon."

So the Companions set off at a brisk pace through the mountains and moorlands of Wales until the thin man gasped bravely, "It is good that at least I carry no surplus weight to slow us down." But he was failing, so Caradoc gave him a ride, and was alarmed to find he weighed little more than David.

When they arrived at the castle at Caerphilly, one look around was enough to show the Companions that their guide had not overstated his case. They were surrounded by amazingly thin people — people whose cloaks wrapped around them three times, people whom Japhet (whose hair tended to get in his eyes) kept mistaking for doorposts. Even the wind of Peregrine's wings was enough to make several of them cave in at the middle and sit down suddenly.

"Everyone I see is about as fat as a pancake," said David. "And the only rhyme I can find for 'thin' is 'sin.' I can't use that. They seem to be good people, and I don't want to hurt their feelings."

"Try 'din,'" suggested Japhet. "It's your specialty." And he scampered out of range.

Thomas ap Thomas ordered a meal prepared in honor of the Companions. It was nothing like the feast Finn of the Fifty Fights had given, but still, the hillsides had been scoured for whinberries, and the last few local cheeses were brought out of hiding, so a respectable amount of food was found. It was served, as always, in the Great Hall. The Companions sat at the High Table, confident of their ability to solve the problem afflicting all the skinny people in front of them. The same skinny people looked hopefully at the Companions, thinking that deliverance might just be at hand.

The food was brought in. The company looked eagerly at the full platters.

The next morning, the Companions remembered that, but nothing else, when they awoke to find the early light streaming onto empty tables and hungry faces.

On the second night, the Companions took more care. For one thing, they were hungry themselves, and for another, they were feeling somewhat foolish. David took his harp into the Hall and settled down to play all his liveliest airs, about lambs frisking in May, and Things that go Bump in the Night. Japhet thumped his tail in time and settled down to count sheep, an activity he felt was guaranteed to keep him awake. Caradoc placed a gong, made by the most inventive blacksmith in Morgannwg, at his right hand. Periodically he struck it, jerking everyone upright with shock. Peregrine, in the rafters, rattled the bells he had attached to his talons, a thing he normally detested. Rhiannon had taken a long nap and was sure she could always stay awake at night.

"Lucky for Thomas ap Thomas I am an owl, not a lark," she murmured.

The whole company took up the idea of keeping

sleep at bay with noise. Knives banged, drinking horns clattered, boots stamped, and many voices took up the chorus of David's songs. Everyone was sure that sleep was quite out of the question, what with bell, gong, harp, and song. The food was brought in. The platters were not quite so full this time.

Everyone was wrong. From the castle to the smallest hut on the hillside, every household slept that night, while their food again disappeared.

When they awoke, the Companions felt dreadful. They were twice as hungry as they had been, and the skinny people of Caerphilly were no longer looking at them with even the slimmest of hopes.

"We should have known that such a rum collection of beasts from the north would be no help at all," muttered someone.

"Thank you for your good will. It was kind of you to come all the way from Caernarfon to try to help us. I am sorry the spell proved too strong for your skills," said Thomas ap Thomas politely. "I hope you have a safe journey back."

"Thank you, but we are not leaving just yet. We will try one last time," said Rhiannon firmly.

The owl thought all the next day. With her head tucked underneath her wings, you might have thought she was sleeping, an unpopular activity in those parts. As a result of her pondering, each Companion was in a different place by evening.

Peregrine perched in an oak tree, high on Eglwy-silan Mountain, from where he could look directly at the comings and goings at Caerphilly Castle, three miles away.

"Let us be thankful for long sight," Rhiannon had said when he protested that he was too far away and wanted to be on the spot with the others. "I promise you this will be more useful than counting the moons of Jupiter."

David and Japhet were directed to the watchtower above the main gate and given the gong that Cara-doc had used to such little effect before.

"Enjoy the one and only time you are likely to be left alone with a gong that can be heard a full fifteen leagues away," Rhiannon said in answer to David's grumbles that he had a better plan, which involved disguising himself as a local sheep.

Caradoc sat at the High Table at the right hand of Thomas ap Thomas. Beside him stood a large bucket of cold water.

"Would you prefer not to look ridiculous, and to let these poor people starve?" replied Rhiannon witheringly, when Caradoc objected that people would laugh at a dragon with his head in a bucket of water. "Besides, find me one creature in Caer-philly who feels like laughing today." Rhiannon herself was perched in the rafters of the Great Hall, directly above Caradoc's head.

At sundown the day's meal was laid as usual

on the tables of all the households in Caerphilly. In the Great Hall, Caradoc reluctantly practiced ducking his head into the cold water. His fire sizzled damply, and he felt downright silly.

David and Japhet arranged themselves, one to keep an eye out for Peregrine's signal and one ready at the gong. Then Japhet insisted on rearranging them so that if they did fall asleep they would fall onto the gong itself. It all required a fair amount of acrobatic skill.

"Well, some good has come out of my Wild Beast of Tartary performances after all," said Japhet, breathlessly, from his final perch on top of David's shoulders.

All the while, Peregrine, from his distant oak tree, watched a great mountain of a man stride down the Rhymney Valley toward Caerphilly. The top of his head rose above the sides of the valley, and with every stride he took, he came half a mile nearer the castle. He had two bags slung over his shoulders. One was so big you could put the River Rhymney itself in nicely and have room to spare. From the other, he scattered handfuls of dust before him, so fine that Peregrine could barely make it out. What he could see was its effect on the dogs and cats, on the birds in the trees and the snails on the walls, and, not least, on the people of Caerphilly. They all fell fast asleep.

The giant worked his way from house to house,

reaching in at each window to scoop up all the food inside and fill his bottomless bag.

"That's the way I like it," he mused to himself in a voice that nearly shook Peregrine out of his tree. "No fuss, no bother, and my food all cooked for me by these friendly little souls in Caerphilly. The food's going downhill, though. Pity. That Midsummer Feast was the best I have ever popped into my little brown bag."

The ducks and drakes were dreaming on the castle moat, and the fish in its waters were asleep in the deep. The giant already had one huge foot on the drawbridge. Peregrine began to panic. He had been quite unable to catch David's sleepy attention with his warning signal. Now he started to fly the three miles to the castle, knowing full well that he could never do it in time. Suddenly, the mighty gong rang out, twice. It woke people from Bristol to Swansea. More important, while two friends were rubbing the bumps on their heads and wondering what had happened, it woke Rhiannon.

Rhiannon struggled with her eyelids once again and managed to open one enough to see an enormous shadow pass the doors of the Hall. She could not have unfurled her wings for love nor money, but this she had expected. Loosening her grip on the oak rafter, she fell from her perch and dug her claws into Caradoc's most tender spot, just behind the ears. Caradoc plunged his head into the bucket of cold water and woke up to see an enormous arm reach in at the window to steal the food from the sleeping company. With his best ear-splitting roar, he breathed a long curl of fire at the huge hand, which was sweeping the table bare. With a shout of pain that should have wakened the Seven Sleepers, but didn't stir the snorers of Caerphilly, the giant dropped his bag and left, nursing his injured hand and bellowing like a hundred calves. While thirty miles away the citizens of Swansea and Bristol, unnerved by the noise, manned the walls and barred the gates, Peregrine thankfully watched the man-mountain take three giant strides up the valley and vanish over the watershed, never to be seen in Morgannwg again.

When the sleepers awoke, for the first time there was food still on their tables. They sent up a cheer, which made Bristol cringe, and set to work with the appetite of people who have had no dinner for forty-four days. When no one could stuff in another mouthful, they hung up the giant's food bag on the watchtower for a trophy. (Later, they stored the gong inside it as a result of the earnest requests of the people of Swansea, who jumped every time some passerby struck the thing.) Then they rang all the bells of Caerphilly, banged the gong, and strummed a battery of harps brought out to sing the praises of the Companions.

Thomas ap Thomas warmly invited them to stay and feast for a month, but the Companions felt that would indeed supply too much surplus weight for a comfortable journey home. Besides, they had other things on their minds. So the people of Caerphilly said regretful farewells before they got down to the serious business of fattening themselves up, and the Companions set out for Caernarfon, where David and Japhet were eager to organize the First Annual North Wales Championship Marble-Rolling, Harp-Plucking, and Gong-Ringing Contest, and Caradoc was eager to fulfill his bargain with Caernarfon before more of the year slipped by.

GREEN APPLES

BEFORE THEY KNEW IT, winter had come to Gwynedd, and by early December the Companions were snug in their cave. The potato harvest had been picked and now lay on the hillside protected by a great mound of oat straw, bracken, and turf, promising winter feasts to come. Caradoc's herbs were drying in neat bundles. The leeks were still in the ground, and so, to Japhet's and David's dismay, were endless rows of cabbages and parsnips. Caradoc looked proudly at the rows of kippers he had smoked. Peregrine hoped he would not be offered any.

"Now we are right and tight for music and storytelling all winter," said David happily, as they hung the last string of onions and got out the marbles.

Japhet knocked three out of the circle on his first roll and tried to look as if he could do that every day. "We were forever moving on with the Wild Beast Show, and I always dreamed of finding a place I would never have to leave. Now that I have, I'm not going to budge from this fireside, or, at the very most, from this hillside, until spring."

Caradoc coughed at the back of the cave, where he was working on a cold remedy. Rhiannon closed her eyes a little tighter.

"None of us can budge until we're sure of the outcome on Twelfth Night," Peregrine reminded the brown dog.

He should have known they were asking for trouble. Sure enough, the next morning Caradoc received an urgent plea from the farthest tip of Gower in the very south of Wales. David of the White Rock, the great blind bard, who had once taught a black lamb to play the harp, sent word asking Caradoc to come at once to cure his sick granddaughter.

"Nothing has helped her," he said. "She is beyond our skills. If you cannot heal her, then no one can."

"But . . ." protested Peregrine in vain.

Caradoc had already begun to collect his herbs, herbals, and remedies.

"I'll go with you to keep you company. Besides, I can't miss a bardic chance like this," said David, wrapping his harp in a heavy linen cover and lambswool for protection on the journey.

"I'll fly with you and spy out the best tracks through the winter mud," offered Peregrine, "so that you can return in good time."

"Since you insist on going, I had better come along," said Rhiannon. "The daylight is so short in December, you will need me to guide you through the dark if you are to make haste to Gower and back again."

Japhet looked at the cheerful fire, hesitated a longing second, and then said bravely, "I will come, too. Perhaps I can make the child laugh, which will help Caradoc cure her."

So they banked the fire and set out for Gower through the gray December drizzle.

They arrived at the lonely settlement, perched at the very end of Gower peninsula above the cliffs called the Worm's Head, on a wet Welsh noon. Below them they could hear the waves breaking on the rocks. From the house there came such lovely music that they were stopped, spellbound. David knew, even better than the others, that only one man in Wales could play like that, and tears started in his eyes at the sadness that was woven through the airs which his old master played. Three otters had splashed up the stream, and two hedgehogs and a badger crept from the wood to hear. The sun suddenly slanted through a gap in the clouds. It seemed impossible that the little girl needed anything more than the harp of David of the White Rock to cure her.

But Gwenno was getting worse, not better. She tossed and turned, refused to eat, and asked crossly for green-and-yellow apples. Her room was full of apples in all colors, shapes, and sizes. There were green Beauty of Bath beside her bed, yellow pippins on the windowsill, rosy pearmains on the chimney-piece. There were baskets full of russets and codlings, Winesaps and Wealthys, Good Christians and Newton Wonders, and many more nameless ones. There were huge apples and small apples, wormy ones and whole ones. There were shriveled ones, fat juicy ones, lumpy apples, bumpy apples, and perfectly smooth apples. The apple trees of Gower and far beyond had been scoured in search of the fruit that would make Gwenno well again. But still she refused them all.

"Yet," said her grandfather sadly, "she keeps on saying that just one taste of green-and-yellow apples would make her well. I long for my sight again, in a way which I have not done for fifty years, to look for this apple."

He led them, feeling for the way, now his granddaughter was not at hand to guide him, to where the child lay, burning one moment and shivering the next.

"Gwenno, tell me about those green-and-yellow apples," invited Caradoc.

The little girl was so charmed to see a friendly dragon at her bedside that she sat up and said, in an almost normal voice, "Well, I am glad somebody asked me at last, instead of bringing me all these silly, ordinary apples. You see, there was an old woman down by the sea, gathering cockles for her supper. She had a cat called Mog. The cockle baskets were heavy, so I helped her carry them over the rocks. She asked me about grandfather and said I was a good girl, and she wished she had someone like me at home to help her. Then she gave me an apple to eat. It was such a pretty apple, as green as emerald on one side and as yellow as brass on the other." She started to toss and turn feverishly.

"How I wish I had that apple now! Won't you

get it for me? I know it will make me well again."

The Companions listened to Gwenno's tale unhappily. It was all too clear to them who the old woman with her cat must be.

"The Black Witch of Carmarthen," explained David to Japhet.

"But this is not Carmarthen," protested Japhet. "This is Morgannwg."

"She is probably plotting to take over all South Wales," said Peregrine, looking on the black side.

Caradoc became more and more concerned during the next week, when none of his herbs and medicines seemed to make the slightest difference to the sick child. She just moved her aching head from side to side and talked all the more of green-and-yellow apples. Japhet tried to cheer her up by turning somersaults. She didn't even smile when he fell flat on his nose attempting a triple backward jump with a sideways spin. Peregrine, keeping a weather eye out for the Black Witch, brought her apples from all the gardens and storehouses of South Wales. David tried to play for her, but she said he made her head ache worse than ever.

On a Friday night before Christmas, they all sat in the stone-flagged, usually cheerful kitchen. Caradoc was worried. Rhiannon was worried. David of the White Rock drummed his fingers anxiously on the table top. He had given up playing the harp because whatever music he started always seemed to end up as a lament. Looking forward was unbearable. No one had the heart to think about Christmas, or indeed anything but Gwenno.

Peregrine was offering to fly to the Wise Woman of Bardsey for advice when the sheep dog by the door and the cattle corgi by the hearth both slunk shivering under the table. The harp in the corner jangled in discord, and the Black Witch herself rapped on the door with her stick and walked in uninvited, followed by a huge marmalade-and-black cat, bristling with menace.

"So," she said, resting her chin on her stick and looking around the frozen room. "To think the poor little girl is sick, and none of these clever animals can find a cure."

She made an unpleasant rasping sound, which Mog alone recognized as a laugh. He stretched his mouth in a frightful grin to match.

"Never worry, my dears. I can cure her. She is a kind little thing, and I have seen how she guides her grandfather around. I have decided that she shall live with me and work for me with her pretty little fingers. Now and then, she shall fetch the old man to play a tune or two for me. And in return I shall feed her the apples she craves. Only they can cure her, and I am the one person in the Western World who knows their secret. I could have saved you all so much trouble, my gooseberry fools, if you had come to me first, instead of shaking every apple tree in South Wales."

Again she rasped, and again Mog's face creased obediently.

"Such a lot of useless apples for you all to eat up, my dears. Ask your friend Caradoc to try frying them for breakfast."

Rasp, rasp, rasp.

"What are you thinking of, old woman?" said the bard, fiercely for such a gentle man. "Gwenno shall never enter your house again and eat your poisoned apples, let alone remain as your slave."

"That would be a pity," said the witch, "because if she doesn't come and eat my beautiful green-and-yellow apples soon, she will not last until Christmas. Such a dear, helpful little girl, too. I am sure you will all miss her sadly."

With that, Mog leaped onto her shoulder, and they turned for the door. She looked round one last time to say: "I am sure you will play a most touching funeral dirge for your granddaughter, old David, but think how much more sensible it would be to give her to me. Then, if you asked nicely, you could come and play music for our supper every night. I am sure this ridiculous brown dog could guide you to us and make himself useful for once."

Then away went the cat and the Black Witch together, down the cliff path.

There was nothing to be said. Everyone went silently to bed, except old David, who took up his harp again, for comfort, and Caradoc, who read and reread his herbals in case he had missed some antidote to poisoned apples, which were as green as emerald on one side and as yellow as brass on the other. Rhiannon, who rarely slept when the others did, kept her grave eyes on the sick child.

"I can't sleep," complained Gwenno. "If I shut my eyes things get smaller and smaller, and then they get larger and larger until they break into pieces inside my head."

Japhet had nightmares, too, about being captured by the Black Witch and forced to lead her everywhere.

"We need a miracle this Christmas," said Peregrine to Rhiannon next morning, when he looked in and saw Gwenno calling deliriously for apples.

"Of course," said Rhiannon. "Bird-witted that I am, not to have thought of it sooner. The Christmas miracle. The Glastonbury Thorn!"

Peregrine looked at her, perplexed. "What's that?"

She explained. "They say that when Joseph of Arimathea came to Britain, he arrived at the place where Glastonbury hill rose like an island among the marshes of Somerset. There he stuck his staff into the ground and set to work to build the first Christian church in this land. The staff took root and grew into a tree, which blossoms only at Christmas. Some say that the flowers of that thorn can work miracles. Surely we should see whether they are powerful enough to counteract the black magic of the Witch of Carmarthen?"

"I will go and get them," said Peregrine simply.

"We will go together," said Rhiannon.

It was a hard flight. The winter storms over the Bristol Channel seemed particularly bad. They wondered if the Black Witch had seen them depart and was using one of her foul-weather spells. The two Companions found the shortest crossing place. From Penarth Headland, they launched themselves right into the gale, and struggled toward a resting place on the tiny island of Steep Holm, where they drew breath again in the shelter of the cliffs, among colonies of outraged gulls. They dared not rest long, in case the witch thought up something worse and they lost the courage to fly on. In any case, the smell of years of gull droppings was enough to make the winds seem sweeter. At last, in the teeth of the wind, they made the shelter of the Somerset coast.

The weather improved once they neared Glastonbury.

"Perhaps it is just Welsh weather that is so bad," suggested Peregrine.

"It is because we are at last out of the Black Witch's spell-casting range," answered Rhiannon, firmly squelching such nonsense.

Dazed and weary, they followed the straight

line of a dike, fringed with willows, across the flat marshes, to where Peregrine could see Glastonbury hill standing up above the surrounding Levels.

The bedraggled pair alighted at the abbey St. Dunstan had founded at the holy place, and explained their mission. They were welcomed, and then warmed, dried, and fed in the abbot's hospitable kitchen, which had huge fires blazing in all four corners.

"Caradoc would be happy here," they said to each other.

The abbot himself took them up onto Wearyall Hill, where the thorn tree was already, three days before Christmas, a mass of blossoms. The abbot broke off a spray and gave it to Rhiannon.

"Go in peace, my friends," he said. "The Holy Thorn is our Christmas miracle. May it work one for the child."

The journey back threatened to be even worse than the one from Wales to Glastonbury. The Black Witch flung sleet, snow, gales, hail, and blinding rain in their direction. But the abbot had been forewarned. He opened the great brown leather Weather Book before they left, and gave them a patch of blue sky to fly under, as far as the tip of Gower.

There, Rhiannon gently squeezed a touch of nectar onto Gwenno's lips. The child smiled her first smile in months.

"That tickles," she said drowsily.

Then, clutching the blossom, she fell at last into a deep, peaceful sleep.

When she awoke, it was as if the dreadful winter had never been. In her absolutely normal, everyday voice, she said, "I'm hungry. What's for supper? I could eat anything but apple tart. Somehow I don't like the idea of that. I think I had a bad dream about it. Who stored all these apples in my room?"

It was too late for the Companions to return to Caernarfon before Christmas, and all of them were secretly pleased to yield to the entreaties to stay and celebrate at Gower.

It was a Christmas Day to remember. The stone-flagged kitchen was cheerful once more, crammed with people and animals. Old David and young

David played some of the happiest music anyone had ever heard, and Gwenno sang for them in her clear soprano. There was storytelling as well as music. The bard told them how he had come by the White Rock part of his name. Peregrine told some awestruck youngsters about hunts at the court of Math, son of Mathonwy. Caradoc told about his dreadful deeds as a young dragon in North Wales (he kept quiet about his old exploits in the south), although he was careful to point out how the hermit had changed all that. Then he did fire-lighting tricks until Rhiannon flew outside to check that the roof was of stone, not thatch. Japhet taught them all the finer points of marble-rolling and told everyone's fortune with the aid of five pebbles. The story, however, that was told over and over again, and that no one got tired of hearing, was of the flight to Glastonbury and the fetching of the thorn.

The only place where there was no celebration was in the lonely cottage below the Worm's Head, where the high tide left flotsam and jetsam at the door. There, the Black Witch of Carmarthen threw some rotting apples out to sea, kicked her cat, and crunched cold seaweed for her Christmas cheer.

"Well, well," said the bard genially. "If the First Day of Christmas is so agreeable, think how festive we shall be here on the Twelfth."

The Companions looked at each other in horror.

How could they have forgotten the trial, which had lain like a dark threshold between the end of this year and the years to come?

The bard smiled affectionately at David. "We shall be glad to have another bard at the Minstrels' Feast."

In the ordinary way, David would have asked nothing more than to be addressed as a bard by the greatest one of them all. Today, however, he was too busy looking for his harp case to let the words fully sink in.

Caradoc hastily explained why they must, at all costs, be back at Caernarfon for Twelfth Night. When Gwenno and her grandfather understood what was at stake, they were overwhelmed at the extent of Caradoc's generosity in coming south at such a time.

So the five friends left, their faces turned apprehensively toward the north, and the sound of the bard's farewell music ringing in their ears.

TWELFTH NIGHT

THE TWELFTH DAY of Christmas dawned damp and gray. Caradoc was half-inclined to use his old mist spells to make both the cave and its inhabitants invisible. However, the thought of explaining such cowardice to his friends sent him instead to collecting firewood.

"One way or another, this will be a Twelfth Night to remember," he rumbled as he heaped more branches on the pile they were making among the ruins of Segontium.

"I hope for one way, but fear it will be the other. A year is surely too short to atone for my ill-spent youth."

The trial was to be held not in the town of Caernarfon, nor on the hillside above, but on the neutral ground of the old Roman frontier town.

"I can't help remembering that the Romans were driven away from this place," confided Japhet to David, as he scampered into the ruined amphitheater with some bracken for kindling.

"Didn't they choose to return to Rome? Something to do with the impossibility of growing grapes in the Welsh rain," said Peregrine, winging in from casting an interested eye on various ships sailing into Caernarfon harbor.

"Well, anyway, the Druids lived here before the Romans," said David from under a load of peat for the fire, with a misty sense of historical accuracy. "I think we count as Druids. We like music and mistletoe and herbs and things. I'm sure they'll ask us to stay."

Japhet was tickled. "I'd happily be a Turkish Druid if only they'd let Caradoc stay."

"Surely they won't drive him out?" asked David, shocked at the idea.

"You never can tell," said Peregrine, taking off again for his guard duty on the Menai Straits.

The day seemed endless, even though the midwinter twilight fell early. By four in the afternoon there was a steady stream of people from Caernarfon looking for a good seat for the evening's drama, not too far from the fire by preference.

Caradoc suddenly found some urgent errands in the cave. For a while Rhiannon watched him stacking the fir cones more tidily, rebraiding a string of onions, and counting his bundles of bay leaves. Then she said, "My friend, before you start patting each scale on that long tail into place, I would remind you that you have done good deeds enough and to spare. Let us go down now together and enjoy the welcome you will receive."

"The trouble is," said Caradoc, at last allowing her to see how worried he was, "I have been counting and recounting, but I cannot find twelve deeds that are sure to satisfy Caernarfon."

"How about finding the Book of Kells?"

"It was little enough to do for Saint MacDara for all his kindness to a waterlogged dragon. Besides, that was in Ireland, and not in Wales."

"You freed me from my fetters on Cadair Idris," Rhiannon reminded him, "an undoubtedly Welsh mountain."

"But that was before the people here had agreed on a term of trial."

"Bless your scales," said Rhiannon, losing some of her habitual reserve. "Haven't we spent the past year rescuing Manx princesses, imprisoning ill-tempered Korean dragons, curing the granddaughters of famous bards, fattening the good people of Caerphilly, and putting fish back on every table in West Wales?"

Caradoc groaned. "Of course, but you are the one who has been reminding me all year that the people of Caernarfon are concerned about what happens in their own town, or at most in the Province of Gwynedd. What have I been about? Spending all my time in Galway, in the farthermost of the Western Isles, in Somerset, and Gower, and the Rhymney Valley? It is on this particular hillside that I wish to dwell in peace for the rest of my lengthy dragon days, and not roaming about the Western World.''

"Piffle,'' said Peregrine, flying in low enough to catch the last sentences. "Good deeds know no geography.''

"Let us hope so, since it is high time I faced my judges and found out their notions of geography,'' said Caradoc, regaining heart from their concern. "It is a comfort that we can go together. This year has certainly taught me that the company of good friends is quite as important as landscapes dear to the heart. Perhaps it is greedy to want both in this life. I must ask Saint MacDara's opinion on that someday.''

David was playing the twenty-fourth verse of "A Falcon in an Oak Tree,'' his new version of "A Partridge in a Pear Tree.'' He stopped as Caradoc appeared in the old Roman arena.

"Bringing that ditty to an end counts as one good deed to my ears,'' growled a bystander.

The crowd fell silent. David tried to nudge it into a rousing cheer with a "hip, hip, hooray'' on the harp, but no one seemed to recognize his hint. The silence confirmed Caradoc's worst fears. His tail felt leaden and dragged behind him as he advanced into the center of the gathering. From force of habit, he gave a fiery breath to get the bonfire going more strongly, and immediately wished he hadn't. It was the worst moment to remind the assembly that, however peaceful his ways, he was still a fire-breathing dragon.

"Harrumph." The spokesman cleared his throat, another old habit, since Caradoc's comfrey poultice had cured his cough last winter.

"Friends, families, and — er — countrybeasts, we are met to decide whether the dragon we see before us has fulfilled his measure of twelve good deeds and is welcome to remain in his native hills, or whether bad memories linger on, and he must now find another home."

Caradoc looked hard into the fire. He had lost his usual air of authority. Peregrine looked up far into the night sky and counted the rings of Saturn to calm his mind. Rhiannon closed her eyes. Japhet opened his ears among the crowd. The speaker went on: "Last time we ate your food, so before we get down to business tonight, we invite you all to share our Twelfth Night cake."

The crowd looked round expectantly as the bakers of Caernarfon staggered in, their knees buckling under the weight of an enormous currant cake. The town swordsmiths set to work, expertly cutting equal slices, which the children distributed. Before long, everyone held a slice of delicious, dark cake in their hands, hoofs, claws, or paws, as the case might be. The chief baker held up his hand for silence.

"As you know, on Twelfth Night each year we hide a lucky bean in the cake. Whoever finds it has a year of good fortune and rules this gathering tonight."

Peregrine took his eyes off the rings of Saturn and fixed them on Caradoc's slice. The dragon had been known to chew the stones of his cherries and crunch the odd shell with his hazelnuts, and certainly could not be relied upon, in his present worried state, to spot a lucky bean in a slice of Twelfth Night cake. Peregrine thought right. He pounced in the nick of time, just as the bean was about to disappear forever into Caradoc's jaws.

"In all my days of hunting for Math, son of Mathonwy, I never made such a swift and accurate dive," thought Peregrine with some pride.

"Give it to me," said Rhiannon softly. Her eyes were still closed, but she had not missed a single rustle of Peregrine's feathers. "Caradoc is in no state to rule tonight. He would doubtless exile himself to Scotland. Who knows but we may help him to that year of good fortune?"

As if to prove her right, Caradoc gave his half-eaten slice of cake to Japhet, saying, "You were right. The Golden Bird needs company. Being alone and friendless for three hundred years is a worse fate than being exiled from the land you love. When they send me away from here, as no doubt they will, I shall join her in the Western Isles."

Rhiannon glided to a perch on what had once been the Roman centurions' bath house, opened the great headlights of her eyes to their fullest, and held up the bean.

"Tu who. This entitles me to ask whether you welcome this noble Welsh dragon to the hillsides of Gwynedd, or whether you will harden your hearts and banish him to lonely exile?"

The people were suddenly shy and looked round for someone to answer. A speaker in a black cloak promptly shuffled forward and sniffed: "I understand that we are all judges here tonight. It is just

as well, because that one," she pointed at Rhiannon, "is clearly partial to this bronze beast." She glared at Caradoc for a moment and then continued.

"I have a list, longer than my arm, of harm done by this mischievous bunch of animals in the last twelvemonth, when at least one of them was supposed to be proving his good will to all. Listen to these crimes:

"First of all, they pulled a feather from a rare bird in its island refuge and imprisoned a Korean dragon far from its native habitat, thus wilfully causing pain and discomfort to wildlife. Next, they deprived the King of Cumbria of his promised bride. Third, they tricked an Irish chieftain out of the best volume in his library. Fourth, they took a branch from a tree that is a national treasure. What would happen, you may well ask, if every pilgrim helped himself to a souvenir of the Glastonbury Thorn in that reckless way? I could keep you here until midnight reciting these animals' shocking misdeeds. They sail in a coracle not registered in their names. They duped some innocent moles out of their gold deposits. I have heard of a very hungry man robbed of his suppers in Caerphilly, and some traveling Tartars treated badly in Chester. I know for a fact that they have persecuted a poor old widow woman and repeatedly deprived her of her means of livelihood and hopes of comfort."

The black hood shook vigorously as it made that last accusation.

"What's more, this so-called reformed dragon and his motley crew have been committing these despicable deeds at a safe distance from Gwynedd. They little guessed that the truth would leak back to Wales before your decision tonight."

It was all a big lie, boldly told, and the crowd looked around with puzzled frowns.

"No," Caradoc told himself, "spitting flames is out. Remember your promise to the hermit." He drew in a deep breath, which almost put the fire out, and then set about rekindling the blaze with tremendous energy.

Rhiannon unfurled her wings, and before the witness, who was watching Caradoc with a spiteful smirk, knew what was happening, she was dragged into the firelight and her hood snatched back by a relentless talon. Rhiannon turned to Peregrine, perched on the topmost stone of what had been the charioteers' entrance: "Explain to the good people in your loudest hunting voice just who our guest is."

Peregrine began almost dreamily. "This day I watched a boat put into Caernarfon harbor from distant Carmarthen. Who was so interested in joining our meeting, I wondered. So I looked a little longer." His voice grew loud and harsh. "Behold the Black Witch of Carmarthen, come to prevent justice tonight."

The crowd recoiled. The reputation of the Black Witch was well known. The cloaked figure slunk away into the shadows, defeated.

"Let me tell you another version of these events," said Rhiannon, and told them.

"Well, I dunno," said one man sourly when she had finished. His stomach hurt, and he had failed to find Caradoc at home to ask him for a cure. "Weren't these good deeds supposed to be done right here in Wales instead of goodness knows where in the Western World?"

Caradoc sank a little lower. He had known this would come.

The Wise Woman of Bardsey spoke up: "No town is an island. Good done to others is done to us."

The fellow hesitated to ask what she meant, in case it was perfectly obvious to everybody else. The crowd lost interest in him and looked instead to where a determined goat was butting its way to the front. Japhet jumped up in excitement and knocked David's harp. David turned the jangle into music for the entry of a long-lost friend. The goat arrived at the fire, plonked two unceremonious hoofs on Caradoc's back in order to see better, and said: "This dragon may not look much, with all these coils and funny-colored scales. He certainly lacks the beauty of a goat, but I tell you he gave me my freedom at Chester Fair when I had given up hope. Now you just let him live where he wants to. He's as Welsh as we are and has as much right to this hill as I have to Mount Snowdon."

The goat marched out, presumably heading back to Snowdon.

"Remember how we found him so smelly we hoped he would go and live miles and miles away from here?" said Japhet, so excited that he was running in circles round David.

"Smelly without, but beautiful within," sang the lamb.

Rhiannon looked over the crowd. "Any other remarks?"

A line of townswomen stood balanced on the low wall, which had once marked the edge of the arena, in order to see over the heads in front of them. Japhet had been listening to them earlier.

"Go on," he urged. "You can't let a goat be braver than you are."

"Right you are," said several voices.

"As if we haven't talked of anything else all year," said one, clambering onto the stump of a ruined column and standing with arms akimbo. "Sorry, Lord Caradoc, if we had a bit more courage, and had spoken up sooner, this ridiculous trial would not be taking place."

Her neighbor turned to the crowd. "I ask you,

what other town in the world has a home-grown dragon looking out for its interests? We're the ones who should be pleading with these animals to stay."

The other women joined in a chorus of approval.

"Remember how they ended the fish famine?"

"Witches may be evil, but, judging by this one, dragons certainly aren't."

"Those fish and chips!"

"Hot water!"

"The falcon warned us that time the Vikings came."

"My goodness, yes. Hot water. I'd take that over any one of your grand good deeds."

"The owl gave me good advice."

"My broth tastes so much better with those herbs Caradoc showed us."

"He can traipse off to Gower or the Isle of Man all he wants. No one else could cure my cough. Big deeds are very well. I'm sure the dragon has done his dozen. But it is the small ones that really count."

"Right. When you try counting those, the dragon has done more than twelve times twelve good deeds."

"The little dog makes me laugh."

"The children love him, too."

"That lamb. He's the one."

And they came forward to a surprised Caradoc with a garland of holly and mistletoe.

"It'd be scratchy on anyone else," said a woman,

slipping the wreath over Caradoc's head, "but on you it looks downright handsome." She gave him a smacking kiss.

Caradoc blinked rapidly, and his rumble of thanks came out a little raggedly. The black lamb came to his rescue, and he was able to compose himself and lick away, with only a slight, telltale sizzle, a tear that was hovering over a holly berry, while David plucked a few notes on his harp.

"Let's hear it for dragons."

His harp was soon joined by another of surpassing beauty. The crowd listened, enthralled, while David of the White Rock played as no one else in the Isle of the Mighty could. He sang of poisoned apples, the Thorn of Glastonbury, and a little girl cured. When he had finished, there was scarcely a dry eye left in the company. Then his grand-daughter led him forward into the firelight. "Since the dragon could not stay with the bard, the bard has come to the dragon. We have always celebrated Twelfth Night above the cliffs of Gower, but this year I think it is fitting that we celebrate among the hills of Gwynedd."

There followed such music and song and rejoicing that no one ever forgot the day when Caradoc was finally welcomed in Gwynedd.

All that winter, while Caradoc daily thawed the ice, and the town water ran piping hot, the people of Caernarfon boasted far and wide in Wales of their extraordinary good luck in having a dragon on the doorstep, so to speak.

The cave soon had a broad path worn up to it by the sick who looked for help from Caradoc's herbs and remedies, by the worried who came to ask Rhiannon's advice, by the children who came to ask Japhet riddles, by the young men who came to ask Peregrine for tips on hunting, and by those who loved to listen to the sweet music of David's harp. The Companions were always ready to share a meal, a fire, and a story with the cold, the hungry, or the lonely who came to the cave above Caernarfon.

In the summer the grateful citizens made a second expedition to the cave. This time they brought the town flag as a gift and made a formal speech to the

Companions, hoping they would continue to bring fame and renown to the community by their permanent residence on the hillside. The Companions returned the honor by presenting David's flag to the town, where it flew merrily for many years, and by promising to stay in Gwynedd.

"So long as fire warms," said Caradoc.

"And grass grows," added David.

"While marbles roll," said Japhet, "and Turkish delights."

"While the winds blow and the water runs," put in Peregrine.

"Until the rain no longer falls on Wales," said Rhiannon with finality.

POST SCRIPT

THESE STORIES come from a durable saga, which helped two small boys endure long midwestern journeys between Indiana and Iowa. The storyteller rummaged in the attics of her mind for Welsh images, because she hoped that these children would always have a soft spot for their mother's country. In authentic attic style, the result is a Celtic jumble of bards, harps, and coracles, lambs and dragons, runes and menhirs, Mount Snowdon and Caerphilly Castle.

The setting is a mythical Celtic world. The "dour realities of time, place and everyday life are softened here by a generous application of wishful thinking," as Jeffrey Ganz says in the introduction to his translation of the tales of Welsh heroes—

137

The Mabinogion (London, Penguin, 1976). Caradoc is rescued and converted by a Celtic saint in the first story, and in the Companions' last adventure, Rhiannon and Peregrine go in search of the Holy Thorn at Glastonbury, which was famous some five hundred years later.

In Wales there is a splendid precedent for a high-handed attitude to the confining bounds of strict historical truth. It is to be found in the Mabinogion. This collection of medieval Welsh tales was largely written down in the fourteenth century, after being recounted for centuries by bards and storytellers. The result is an endlessly fascinating and baffling series of scraps and glimpses of Welsh myth and legend, heroes and history, customs and folklore, and indeed almost anything else one cares to look for. The Mabinogion is the source of many ideas in these tales of Caradoc and his Companions.

Some unlikely facts in the Caradoc stories are historically true. St. MacDara, for example, was a real sixth-century Christian missionary, who lived on a sixty-acre island four miles off the southwest coast of County Galway. You can still see the enormous stones in the ruined walls of the church he built there. Admittedly, the fact that a dragon, converted by his good example, shared the island with him for a while has escaped historical record. The Book of Kells, widely considered the supreme achievement of Irish art, was in fact stolen from the sacristy of the church at Kells in 1007 and later recovered. It is not clear how. St. Patrick was known to give gold chalices to the churches he consecrated. At least fifty have been traced. And it is certainly true that the coasts of Britain were constantly attacked, from the late eighth century until the tenth century, by Vikings, who were as notorious for burning churches as they were for plundering the land. David of the White Rock is one of the most famous bards in Welsh history, and a Black Witch makes her appearance in the Mabinogion. However, starting with these historical facts, this car-born bard has taken a creative approach to history and written, as the Celts often do, of what ought to have happened, rather than what actually did.

The stories are more firmly rooted in geography than they are in history, as the map may tell you. Wales covers some eight thousand mild, damp, hilly square miles of western Britain. You can fit it comfortably seven times into Iowa. Rain is a frequent and persistent fact of Welsh life. In places in the northwest the rainfall rises to over a hundred inches a year. The cloudiness and rain in the stories is no exaggeration. The country is high, but not really a mountain land. There are a few isolated peaks at three thousand feet or more, notably Snowdon and Cadair Idris, but the land for the most part is high moorland. Until the Industrial Revolution changed the pattern (and these stories are distinctly preindustrial), the Welsh people clustered in the more fertile valleys and on the narrow coastal plains, where poor harvests could be eked out by fishing. With the sole exception of the cave above Caernarfon, the places in the stories are all real. You can see them for yourselves.

It is easy to imagine a legendary Celtic world lying behind the present-day face of Wales, soaked by the rain into its hills and valleys. Although these stories are no quarries from which to hew the authentic rocks of Welsh history, I hope they give you a glimpse of those older landscapes and leave you, too, with a soft spot for Wales.

the welsh names
and places

THE WELSH LANGUAGE is still spoken by about a quarter of the population, particularly in North and West Wales. Almost all the place names and many of the personal names in the country are Welsh. At first they may look mysterious to the English-speaker (and -speller). If you have ever seen the long name of a small village in Anglesey, Llanfairpwllgwyngyllllantysiliogogogoch, you will probably have given up in despair. In fact the words are not difficult to pronounce, given a few guidelines.

Consonants: Most are as in English. A few differ, notably:

C—always hard, as in *car*.

Ch—as in Ba*ch* (the composer), never as in *ch*eese.

Dd—like *th* in English *th*is.

F—like English *v*.

G—always hard, as in *g*o, never soft, as in *g*entle.

Ll—no English equivalent. Put the tip of your tongue against the roof of your mouth and breathe out, imagining all the time that you are a Welsh goose. Alternatively, give up and use *l* as in *l*amb.

R—is always rrrolled.

Vowels: The vowels are generally sounded as in French. The major spelling problem is solved when you realize that there are two additional vowels:

W—like *oo* in c*oo*l.

Y—a bit more complicated. Generally, *u*, as in *u*ntil.

In Welsh words, the stress is usually on the next to last syllable: Car ad' oc.

Aberdovey (Aber dove' ee): *Aber* means mouth of a river, the River Dovey in this case. A Welsh legend has a drowned town nearby, whose bells can still be heard under the waves of Cardigan Bay.

Angharad (Ang har' ad): means much loved. The *g* is soft as in san*g*.

Ap: Like Mac or O' before a name, it indicates "son of." Thomas ap Thomas means Thomas the son of Thomas.

Bardsey Island: at the western tip of Gwynedd,

famous for the twenty thousand Celtic saints said to be buried there.

Caernarfon (Kair nar' von): *Caer* means fort. Arfon was the name for the region between the mountains of Snowdonia and the coast. To the Romans, it was Segontium, the extreme northwestern outpost of their empire. The town today is overshadowed by the splendid castle built in the thirteenth century by the English king Edward I to subdue the wild Welsh.

Caerphilly (Kair fill' y): the fort of Fili. Fili was one of the less famous sixth-century Celtic saints. The town is known for its cheese and for one of the most magnificent thirteenth-century castles in Britain.

Cantref (Kan' trev): an old division of land, like the present county.

Caradoc (Kar ad' ock): means amiable. In the Mabinogion, he was one of the brave princes who could never be overcome. Another famous Caradoc (in Latin, Caractacus) was the leader of the Britons against the Romans.

Coracle (Kor' ah kul): a light boat made of skins stretched over a frame of willows, used from prehistoric times to the present in some parts of Wales. The Irish version was the curragh, in which St. Brendan was said to have sailed across the Atlantic in 570.

Cumbria (Kum' bre ah): the name for the English

Lake District, just north of Wales on the west coast. The name is related to Cymru, the Welsh name for Wales.

David: in Welsh, Dewi or Dafydd. From the Hebrew; means darling or friend. A common name in Wales since David (who died about 588) became the national saint.

Der-ywch (Dare' ooch): the traditional Welsh way to call animals, especially cattle. Probably a very ancient pre-Celtic word.

Eglwysilan Mountain (Egg loose eel' an): *Eglwys* means church. Ilan was a seventh-century Celtic saint. The area is a high moorland common, just north of Caerphilly.

Gower (rhymes with power): a peninsula of outstanding natural beauty in South Wales.

Gwynedd (Gwin' eth): the old northwest kingdom, which lasted roughly from the seventh to the thirteenth century. The modern county is somewhat smaller, although it includes the traditional counties of Anglesey, Merioneth and Caernarfonshire.

Llanarth (Llan' arth): *Llan* means church. A pretty village on the main highway around Cardigan Bay.

Lleyn (Lean is near enough): the peninsula forming the northern side of Cardigan Bay. Bardsey Island is at its tip.

Llyn Perys (Lin Per' iss): *Llyn* means lake or pool.

One of the twin lakes of Padarn and Perys, in the midst of Snowdonia.

Mabinogion (Mab in og' eon): The title given to a collection of eleven medieval Welsh stories. Mabinogi generally means the tale of a hero's early years. These tales are a mixture of history, folklore, myth, and mistakes.

Math, son of Mathonwy (Math on' we): a legendary figure, Lord of Gwynedd and one of the great heroes of Welsh folk tales.

Menai Straits (Men' eye): the blue water between the island of Anglesey, or Môn, and the mainland of Wales. It was crossed by a remarkable suspension bridge in 1826.

Menhir (Men' heer): from the Welsh meaning long stone. A tall, upright standing stone of great antiquity, found especially on the western fringes of Europe.

Môn (Moan): the older name for the island of Anglesey, traditionally one of the most fertile parts of Wales.

Morgannwg (More gan' oog): the old kingdom of southeast Wales, roughly the present counties of Glamorgan.

Peregrine: a falcon. As a personal name, it means traveler. From the Latin *peregrinus*.

Preseli Hills (Pres el' ee): Also called Mynydd Prescelly. A range of ancient hills in Southwest

Wales ending in the wild coastline around Strumble Head. The famous blue stones for Stonehenge were taken from here.

Rhiannon (Rhee an' non): In the tales of the Mabinogion, she was the beautiful wife of the Prince of Dyfed, famous for her birds, whose notes were so sweet that warriors remained spellbound.

Rhymney (Rum' nee): a river running through the mining area of Southeast Wales.

Snowdon: 3560 feet; the highest summit in Wales. The name is also applied to the whole mountain area of North Wales, which is now the Snowdonia National Park. The Welsh name for both the peak and the area is Eryri (abode of eagles).

Strumble Head: a windswept peninsula with tremendous cliffs and prehistoric remains scattered everywhere.

Teifi (Tye' vee): the chief river of West Wales.